First Printing Lock 'n Load Publishing Paperback Edition 2019
Copyright © 2019 Lock 'n Load Publishing, LLC.
All Rights Reserved.
Printed in the United States of America in the State of Colorado
Lock 'n Load Publishing LLC
1027 North Market Plaza, Suite 107 - 146
Pueblo West, Colorado, 81007
Rev 13
ISBN: 9-781733-104104

D1319609

CONTENTS

INTRODUCTION

First Strike is, at its heart, about the problems of command. The stories told herein are about imperfect people operating under pressure with incomplete information. Some of the decisions these people make are heroic while others are downright questionable. I have tried to paint a picture of human beings at war while at the same time writing with the spirit of the "World at War '85" game itself. If you read between the lines, you'll see the fumbled to-hit rolls, the "End Turn" cards being pulled too early, and the problems of a bad scenario setup.

I have made a faithful effort to recreate the capabilities of weapons that were fielded at the time of the conflict's setting. I also used online maps to gain an understanding of the terrain where these fictional battles were fought. To help gain a rough understanding of how the battles might go, I set up the forces in a computer simulation game called "Armored Brigade" and played things out.

Despite these efforts, the stories are not an attempt to faithfully depict every single aspect of combat and military operations and those who are looking for it may be disappointed with the contents of this book. For the sake of enjoyment and ease of reading, the story must sometimes trump realism.

The book is populated by a host of different characters. Some of them are based on characteristics real people while others were conjured from imagination alone. It almost goes without saying that no offense is intended to anyone who finds their name herein. I have never met or interacted with most of you in any way that would warrant any assumptions about your personal character. For those I happen to know well, I think you'll agree that I was surprisingly gentle on you. You owe me a beer, by the way.

I have no doubt that some readers will find the structure of this book to be a little disjointed. There are no recurring characters and few obvious common threads that can be pulled through the stories. Taken as a whole, the stories serve as a kind of snapshot of what was happening in the Fulda Gap during the very early stages of World War III. These three battles served as the harsh lessons in modern warfare that determined how the war would proceed and ultimately, how it would end. No, that's not a spoiler.

It is my hope that the reaction to this book will be positive enough to warrant subsequent volumes that will build further upon these events to give an overall picture of the war's progress. In other words, this a marathon instead of a sprint. Thanks for running with me.

Sincerely,

Brad Smith
April 2019

ACKNOWLEDGMENTS

I would like to thank Keith Tracton and David Heath for their encouragement and faith in this book. The feedback was immensely helpful and made the final product much better than it otherwise would have been. I am also grateful to my wife, Maya, who gave me the time and space to sit down and get to work. Thanks to my son, Hiro. You were my source of energy and inspiration. I am so proud of who you are becoming. Thank you to Marc von Martial and his excellent illustrations that bring the book to life.

Last but not least, I would like to thank the people who bought the book and took a chance on a fledgling author with their time and money.

The terrain in this book was based on many resources and satellite imagery. There are certainly discrepancies between these recent depictions and what existed in 1985 although the salient geographical features are basically the same.

The battles in this book were modelled by from the many table top and computer wargames I have played over the years. One computer simulation called "Armored Brigade" from Veitikka Studios was extremely helpful. This added much to my understanding about the pace of modern warfare and the problems of clear communication and command.

Books that were immeasurably helpful in the writing and research phase included Michael Green's "M1 Abrams Tank", Mike Guardia's "The Fires of Babylon: Eagle Troop and the Battle of 73 Easting", Tom Clancy's "Armored Cav", and Russell Phillips' excellent reference series, "Weapons and Equipment of the Warsaw Pact."

STORMING THE GAP
FIRST STRIKE

A WORLD AT WAR 85 NOVEL

BRAD SMITH

WARNING SHOTS

January 1981
The Oval Office
Washington, D.C.

"Jelly bean, Keith?"

"No thank you, Mr. President. I'm fine."

"Dave?"

"Ah sure. Why not? Thank you, sir."

"The licorice ones are the best."

The three men settled down on the soft cream-colored couch that dominated the center of the room. The portraits of past presidents hung on the walls, their heavy gaze pressing upon them, silent witnesses to history.

Keith Tracton placed a pair of sweating palms on his lap and braced himself for what was to come next. It was not the high office that had him worried - this was not the first president he had met face-to-face. In fact, his service to the country had demanded three such meetings before. All of them had taken place right after the pomp and ceremony of Inauguration Day had died down. Each new president, swamped with the duties of having to steer the ship of state, had reacted differently to the desperate message that he had to deliver.

It was not a task he had relished, but as the deputy director of the NSA, he had no choice but to pass on his expert analysis of this terrible situation and let the president decide what to do with it. Today, as usual, he had come here with David Heath, the Deputy Director of Operations for the CIA. Hopefully, the two allies could make their voices heard. But Tracton didn't hold his breath.

Nixon hadn't listened. At the time, he was focused too tightly on Vietnam to see the bigger picture. Ford had shrugged and asked what to do. The man had been handled a fumbled ball and didn't expect to be in office long enough to worry about what he considered to be some grand conspiracy theory. Carter was fascinated and made some early efforts to deal with the Russians, but then the gas shortages and Iran happened. By the time the Soviets were in Afghanistan, there wasn't much to do about it except express the country's outrage. The elections came upon them, and Jimmy Carter's fate was sealed.

If there was one word that could sum up the last three presidents, it was this one – distracted.

The pace of the modern world seemed to increase each year. The demands placed on elected officials had outgrown their ability to deal effectively with crises.

This new president seemed to recognize that and had gotten into office on promises of reducing government involvement in ordinary citizen's lives. At the same time, he had vowed to deal with the growing threat posed by the Soviet Union. Maybe this time, the president would listen and act. There was always hope the world could be saved if the right people just stopped for a minute and absorbed what he was trying to say.

"So I understand you're here to bring me up to speed with what's happening in the world?" said Reagan.

The words slid out in that smooth actor's voice. Although Tracton hadn't voted for the man, he could see why others had. The new president had a relaxed and agreeable manner. As he spoke, it was impossible not to feel that everything was going to turn out all right. It wasn't just that you liked the guy. You wanted to like him.

Heath set down the coffee cup and adjusted his tie before clearing his throat. This was part of the ritual, and this is how it always began.

"Mr. President, it's more than just that. The reason we've come here today is to urge you to focus the administration's efforts against a grave and ongoing global crisis. We're here to discuss what's been happening with the Soviets."

At the drop of the final word, Reagan leaned forward. Tracton tried not to get his hopes up too much, but it appeared that he was at least interested in what Heath was about to say.

"The situation, Mr. President, is much worse than it seems. More dangerous than it looks. For thirty-five years now, we've been at war."

Reagan nodded. "I understand we're in a conflict right now… but isn't it overselling it a bit to say 'war,' Mr. Heath?"

"I mean exactly that, Mr. President. The Soviet Union has not only funded but orchestrated and participated in acts of war against this nation and its allies for nearly four decades. Although most of our citizens and politicians are well aware of our mutual enmity, what they don't know is the true extent of the conflict. The fact is that many hostile acts have been committed against the United States and its allies."

The senior statesman put his palms up. "I think I understand what you're saying. I even campaigned on it. But you're right - I'm sure I don't know the full extent of what's happening out there. So can you tell me the history, as you understand it?"

Heath gestured at Tracton, who reached into his briefcase and extracted a thick manila folder. Crammed between its frayed covers were photos, documents, and dossiers. It was a lifetime of work from a thousand different sources - deep cover agents, electronic intercepts, satellite reconnaissance, just to name a few.

"I've got all those documents lined up for your review," said Heath. "But I'll touch on a few details. It started in '46 with the Russians stealing the elections in Romania. The next year, they did it again in Poland."

Tracton jumped in next. "We then pulled off a coup of our own in June '47 with Werner von Braun and the other German rocket scientists. We helped them escape from right out under their noses. Excellent work by our agents."

Reagan nodded along with each beat of the briefing. Heath spoke up next.

"We also sent in a strike team against a small Soviet force. It's uh…neutralization…allowed us to take the German scientists to the States. This, in turn, helped us to advance both our space and nuclear arms programs.

"In February 1948 in the middle of these events, the Soviet sent agents into Czechoslovakia pulling off a coup d'état allowing the Communist Party to take full control. This should never have been allowed to happen, and it was totally the failure of our own agencies. Of course, instead of pushing our advantage, our operations were discouraged and restricted."

With our hands tied domestically, the Soviets were able to insert spies into our nuclear program. They stole many details of our atomic secrets and proved just how much of a worthy opponent they were. By 1949, the Soviet Union detonates its first nuclear weapon."

Reagan clasped his hands together. "I understand completely. I also knew about communist subversion going on back in Hollywood. People called it a 'witch hunt' back then, but some of those people were getting paid a lot of money from foreign governments. Go on, then."

Heath swung back into the early Cold War history lesson. "In May 1948, the Middle East was officially put into play with the birth of Israel. With a few simple words, David Ben-Gurion declared 'the establishment of the Jewish state of Israel.' This turned the whole region into an ongoing conflict."

"Hard to believe how they managed to hold on in those early years," said Reagan.

Heath chuckled. "Well, during the battle for control of Jerusalem, many Arab soldiers claimed that Israel had fighting men falling from the sky. Some said they looked like angels. So we don't know what to make of that, but if God is fighting for them, I guess they got very little to worry about."

On and on the briefing went, touching on the back-and-forth covert conflict that had been the hallmark of the last thirty-five years. Reagan showed minimal surprise. He already knew most of it. By the time they reached the early 1960s, the president looked as if he were ready for a nap. The coffee had been filled and refilled. Tea had been offered and rejected. More than once, the spry septuagenarian had glanced at the clock. By this time, all the other presidents had excused themselves with a polite word or two. The two advisors had never gotten this far before.

Tracton braced himself for what was about to come.

"Sir, there's something you need to know about what happened to Kennedy," he said.

Tracton laid a grainy black and white photograph that showed a man in a dark suit and sunglasses in a shooter's stance with a raised long rifle. In front of him was a grassy knoll.

"This was taken November 22nd, 1963. The day Kennedy died. Many of us think the man in the photo is Andrei Petrinska. A Bulgarian national who is confirmed to have worked for the Bulgarian security services at the time of the assassination. We can't find any direct proof, but three years ago he was contracted by the KGB. He disappeared a week later."

Reagan froze. The temperature in the Oval Office seemed to drop twenty degrees. A hard unmoving silence draped the room as the allegation hit full force.

"You mean to tell me the Soviets shot Kennedy?"

It was Heath's turn to talk. "Not everyone is convinced of that," he said. "But what we do know is they've murdered countless others, Mr. President. They've even killed our servicemen."

Tracton plucked four photographs from the folder and slid them toward the president.

"What am I looking at here?" asked the president. His energy had returned now. Instead of the sluggish silence of the last ten minutes, his eyes brimmed with fiery indignation.

"The first two are ours – the USS Thresher and Scorpion. The next one is Israeli. That's the Dakar. And this final one is the Minerve. It's a French sub. All of them were sunk."

Reagan studied each photograph and set them down gently on the table.

"Sunk? By the Russians?"

Tracton nodded. "The public was never informed of the real reasons, but radio logs and reliable human intelligence have confirmed that hostile action took them down."

By the time they had brought Reagan up to date on the latest events - Afghanistan, Iran, and Nicaragua, the old man looked nearly apoplectic. Clearly, the briefing had had its intended effect. The man wasn't just focused - he was downright angry. Heath pressed on.

"There does seem to be a pattern to this as a whole. The Soviets have not been able to catch us on the technology front but not from the lack of trying. As the tech gap widens, they seem to get more and more brazen. They fall back on their existing strengths - the biggest one being massive numbers. Our guess is the buffer makes them feel safe or at least comfortable. We are working on new weapon designs, and it could very well tip the balance in a way that is uncomfortable for the Soviets to accept. Most recently, they've deployed intermediate missiles into Eastern Europe to counter our cruise missile advantage. These missiles can reach their targets within six minutes."

Reagan turned bright red. He was clearly uncomfortable with the way the initiative had shifted over the recent years.

"Are you suggesting we pull back? I'm not okay with sitting on our keesters and hoping this all goes away."

Heath jumped on the grenade.

"Some of your predecessors have talked about "acceptable levels" of state-sponsored terror. Others have talked about hitting back. But not nearly at the right level required to deter it. And, in my opinion, not in the right ways or places. At the covert level, we advise a much more aggressive approach. Keith and I call it 'low-intensity warfare.' These are militarized covert operations designed to achieve political objectives. They take longer and they can get… messy…but we'll avoid situations like we had in Vietnam. We also recommend accelerating the time frame for the overhaul of our military into a professional volunteer force."

Reagan stood up and wandered over to the large window that looked out onto the White House rose garden. He hovered there for a long moment with his back to them and without turning, spoke in a solemn tone.

"Some of the things I say in my speeches about them – I know they're a bit oversimplified. Good versus evil. Things like that. But I want to know - why? What is this strange human compulsion we have to interfere with the natural way of things? To deny other human beings their basic rights?"

Tracton tucked the folder back into his briefcase. Would it be here again in another four years or would the world be gone by then? It all depended on this one man standing at the window. His next words were solemn and slow, just like truth always came out.

"As far as we can figure out, sir…a lot of it has to do with internal politics. This system they've built. It's on pretty shaky ground. So why not destabilize other countries too? The other part of it is the desire to push things as far as they can go. Break enough rules so that rule-breaking seems normal and acceptable. Establish a new pattern of what's considered 'normal' when really, it's just all part of a messed-up system that works in your favor. The wheels are coming off though. They can't hold on much longer."

Reagan stood up and paced over to his desk. His eyes wandered up to the large oil-painting of Lincoln.

"So things are worse than I thought. Much worse, I suppose. The question is what to do about it. I'll work as hard as I can to counter everything they're doing. Every step of the way, they'll meet resistance. This country's not gonna be pushed around anymore."

Tracton smiled. Finally, someone was getting it. "Sir, I think that's the best news we've heard for quite some time. Please remember this when you're appointing your cabinet."

"What's the danger of this all blowing up in our faces?" asked Reagan. "Can this thing really turn into a war?"

Heath folded his arms and looked at the carpeted floor. "Their economy is a wreck, sir. They've been pumping every last ruble into defense in the last five or six years. Right now, they're putting out weapons at a rate that we'd need at least half-a-decade to match. Things are…not good. The longer this goes on, the greater the danger of something awful happening."

Reagan grabbed some jelly beans and walked around his desk, "You know fellows, Brezhnev is an old time, hard-line Communist I don't see anything changing anytime soon.

On the other hand, maybe we get lucky, and someone else will come along, and we can work with him."

Tracton wasn't so sure. It was good to be optimistic, but it was hard to imagine things getting better. History had shown that systems built on shaky foundations tended to collapse in catastrophic and unpredictable ways. He doubted that Reagan could totally influence the way the Soviet empire ended and he suspected that the Soviets couldn't control it either. The whole country had grown into a machine with a life of its own, spiraling out of control and lurching forward on momentum alone.

Soon, the Russian economy would give out, and the bill would come due. Whether it was paid in blood or riches, no one could say. Doing nothing was not a solution, but the effects of the collapse might be contained with a robust American foreign policy and a lot of luck.

A few minutes later, both Tracton and Heath walked down the long tunnels that led to the Capitol building. The rest of the day would be spent dealing in mundane meetings with Congressmen and Senators about budget allocations, mandates, and oversights. The life of a Washington bureaucrat never stopped or slowed down --- even with the danger of a Third World War looming.

"Do you think he got the message?" asked Tracton.

"Time will tell," shrugged Heath. "I'll say this though – we got a lot further with this one than the others. There's still a glimmer of hope left."

"Let me ask you something," said Tracton. "I know you know things. How long do you really think we've got until this thing explodes into something beyond our control?"

"I'd give us four --- maybe, five years tops."

THE LIBERATORS

December 1984
The Kremlin

Military Industry Secretary Grigory Romanov faced the row of men sitting at the long oak table and scanned their faces for any signs of doubt. Could they be trusted? Their very lives were at stake, and if even one of them were to talk about today's proceedings, the rest of them would face a firing squad before the week was out. Foreheads lined with the same concern stared back at him through the thick fog of cigarette smoke. If any of them harbored an intent to betray the group's existence to the authorities, their face did not show it. Satisfied, Romanov lifted a finger and spoke.

"Each of you is here tonight because you were chosen. Chairman Andropov looked for men who understood that Mother Russia was in great danger. You alone had the insight to know that the West is busy plotting our destruction and that the time for action will come soon," he said. "Tonight, we will decide - once and for all how we will carry out that task. The decisions we make tonight will set the course of history for the coming century. I want you all to speak frankly. If there is something you wish to say, this is the time for it."

A string of wet coughs punctured the silence. Romanov continued.

"The easy victories of the past are over. No longer can we count on the West to indulge in the illusion of so-called 'peaceful co-existence.' The relationship between our countries is in free-fall, and the Americans are no longer willing to pay any price to avoid a conflict. In fact, they are actively working towards a final showdown. As it did forty-five years ago, the decadence of capitalism has fallen prey to the easy answers of fascism. Once again, it falls to us to stamp out this plague before it spreads across the world and kills millions."

Marshall of the Soviet Union Vladimir Orgarkov, the newest member of this secret society, spoke up in his baritone voice. It was the same one that commanded the General Staff.

"No doubt the West has taken a more aggressive stance these last few years. How can you be so sure they are trying to destroy us now? I ask not out of disbelief. I only wish to understand if your reasoning is the same as mine."

Romanov took the question in stride. Men like Orgarkov did not get into such a high office by reckless abandonment of their reason. If the Soviet Union was going to war, such an act should be taken in good faith with regards to facts and evidence. He expected no less from this man. He sipped the hot tea and savored the slight scalding sensation in his mouth. The answer came ready to Romanov's tongue.

"The evidence is clear enough," he said. "In the last three years alone, countless new Western initiatives have been developed with the single goal of thwarting Communist ambitions everywhere."

His fingers flicked up one by one as he spoke. "The Strategic Defense Initiative. Astronomical military budget increases. Pershing II missiles stationed in Europe. The invasion of Grenada. Support of insurgents in Afghanistan. Need I continue?"

Orgarkov grunted as his chin dipped once in agreement. The sour look on the man's face hinted at his resentment towards the West about Afghanistan. The Americans had directly interfered in the Soviet sphere of influence and hadn't even tried to deny it. How many of the Red Army's operations had been thwarted by a single one of those primitive cave-dwellers with a Stinger missile? Too many to count.

One of the younger ones raised a tentative hand. He was among the five junior members of the Politburo who remained unwavering in their support of Soviet Communism. Though naive in their outlook, they listened and did what they were told. Several of the older men here had argued against their inclusion in the group, but Romanov had managed to sway them. The truth was that this group needed new blood. Half of its original members were in the cold ground.

Romanov addressed him with a tone that made it clear he was already stretching things by speaking up. "Yes, Maksim Borisovich? You wish to say something."

"Everything you say is true," said the young man. "But several politicians in the West have talked repeatedly about ensuring peace between our countries. Of course, I do not believe such filthy capitalist lies. But these speeches are used by Gorbachev's supporters to gain support. How are we to counter such arguments?"

Major General Toporov, the commander of the 7th Guards Airborne Division, cleared his throat and gave a contemptuous snort of laughter.

"Words of peace?" he said. "Look at what the American president has said about us in his speeches! Just last year, he called us an 'evil empire'! When we neutralized a spy plane that violated our eastern borders, the reckless stooge called it an act of 'barbarism.' Do I need to replay the tape recording of his so-called 'joke' about bombing us during a national radio broadcast?"

Borisovich stared at the table red-faced and muttered in a weak act of defense. "True…but they are merely words, comrade."

Toporov pushed a pointed finger down onto the table's glassy surface. His face wrenched in white-hot fury.

"Rubbish!" he shouted. "You are too young to remember the mere 'words' that another fascist used to describe us forty-five years ago. The men in this room - the real men - know what it was like to listen to the mad ravings of Adolf Hitler as he denounced us and called for the extermination of the Soviet Union even before 1941. Of course, the rhetoric was dismissed as just that. But if we had only listened, we would have understood that war was upon us before the first fascist crossed our sacred borders.

We would have prepared for the whirlwind of death and violence that was to sweep across our land. Oh, young one! If there is one thing that we learned from those days, it was to listen to your enemy and anticipate his intentions. Act before he can. Did you not grow up in a city without fathers?"

The young man's face reddened at the last statement and Romanov could not help but feel bad for him. After all, Borisovich hailed from Leningrad, a city that had suffered most bitterly from the years-long German siege. It was time to bring the emotions under control now. Toporov's antics might play well in front of a thousand paratroopers who were looking for a reason to die, but they didn't impress this audience.

"Enough," said Romanov. "You have made your point, Comrade Toporov. I am sure that Comrade Borisovich was only asking questions - just as I had requested. We may have our differences but rest assured we are all united in our opposition to the imperialists and our conviction that they are planning something. The NATO exercise last year - "Able Archer" - was proof enough of their intentions to launch a surprise nuclear attack. Operation RYAN confirmed this along with East German intelligence reports. It was clear in its conclusions."

Vladimir Kryuchkov cleared his throat, a clear indication that the KGB's First Chief Directorate and the architect of RYAN wished to talk. Silence descended like a blanket, and the temperature in the room seemed to drop a hundred degrees. Romanov caught himself taking a step back from the man. There was something about him that made everyone squirm.

"Do not talk about RYAN in the past tense, comrade," he said. "It is not finished. It has merely shifted into a new phase. No longer is the aim of the operation to find out if an attack is being prepared on the Soviet Union. Its main objective is now to decide when this nuclear Barbarossa will be launched."

Romanov waited for Kryuchkov to reveal more, but the sentence was left to hang there like a man on a cliffside. Such were the tight-lipped habits of spies who lived to retirement age. Romanov gestured towards Kryuchkov again, daring to push for more information.

"And your conclusions, comrade?"

Kryuchkov opened the leather-bound portfolio case in front of him and slid a pair of thick glasses over a bulbous drinker's nose.

"Reliable estimates indicate they will strike in the second half of 1986. By then, their strategic missile deployment will have reached approximately 10,000 ICBMs. The so-called "Peacemaker" missile will begin deployment early in that year. The basic infrastructure for the Strategic Defense Initiative will be operational in January when Space Shuttle Challenger releases its payload, an advanced tracking and data relay satellite. We already have a team in place that is working to prevent this."

The man's words hinted at something deeply sinister. Romanov was tempted to probe further but the moment passed as Kryuchkov kept talking.

"At the same time, American engineers will have finally perfected the internal guidance system for their AGM-86B cruise missile. It will have unrivalled accuracy against our silos and military command posts. Delivery systems will be in place on land, sea, and air. Looked at individually, none of these is a concern. It is only when one sees all the pieces of the puzzle that the same shocking conclusion must be reached."

With the sheet tucked back into his portfolio case, Kryuchkov folded his arms and leaned back in his chair.

A shudder swept across Romanov's legs. He sat down in the plush leather chair and struggled to find the words that needed to be said.

Orgarkov anticipated the question before it could be asked. The broad-shouldered military man clasped his hands.

"The Red Army is prepared to act to prevent this," he said. "If the Politburo wills it, we will send our men and tanks across the borders with our enemies and seize them by the throat before they eradicate us like rats. It can be done - if surprise can be achieved."

Could Russia be saved in time? Romanov wanted so badly to believe this man. He turned to Admiral of the Fleet Sergey Gorshkov, who had yet to say anything.

"Admiral, everyone here respects your opinion. What do you have to say to these proceedings? I beg you to speak openly."

Each word creaked out of the 75-year-old admiral.

"I am aware of Marshall Ogarkov's covert efforts to upgrade the Red Army's training and equipment these past ten years. While the attention of the world was transfixed by our revolution in Soviet naval affairs, he spearheaded efforts to modernize the land forces. Whatever measures are taken to prevent the imperialists from destroying the motherland, the ships and submarines of the state will be there to support its aims. As always, the navy stands by ready to act."

Toporov spoke next. "So it is agreed. We rain fire down on the capitalist cities and scorch their lands. Then we roll west and destroy whatever remains. The world will be changed certainly, but our descendants will thank us for giving them a world without fear of fascist invaders."

Romanov jumped in. Things were going in a new and most unwelcome direction now. The idea of launching a nuclear strike was madness. He had seen the photos of radiation survivors after Hiroshima and Nagasaki. No one deserved such a cruel death.

"Let us not be too hasty with our assumptions," he stammered. "A nuclear conflict would be unpredictable and dangerous for both sides. Millions of our own would die too. The land would be poisoned for generations. Let us not forget, general - this is the very thing we are trying to prevent."

Gorshkov and Orgarkov nodded in unison. Their lives had been dedicated to studying and understanding the implications of using such weapons. Seeing that his superiors were against the idea, Toporov threw his hands up and stammered out an excuse.

"I was - was only trying to explore options, comrades. I'm sure you understand."

Romanov smoothed things over with a shrug.

"Of course, general. That is exactly what we are here to do. Explore options. We all agree, however, that capitalism as a force in the world must be abolished completely and that these are the central war aims. Nothing less than the total and unconditional surrender of the United States and its allies must be achieved by its end. Launching a nuclear attack is certainly within our capabilities - but I urge you to imagine what it would be like instead to humiliate the Americans at every turn. To see them crushed utterly."

The men at the table said nothing. Romanov took it as silent consent. As if by some miracle, a consensus had been reached that the West was a threat and needed to be dealt with very soon by conventional military force. The only question left was how it could be pulled off. The rest of the details would be determined later on.

"So then, gentlemen," said Romanov. "We know what to do and when. This project must be conducted with utmost secrecy. There is also the problem of Gorbachev. If he attains ultimate political power, all this is for nothing."

Tokarov's hands shot up. The man was clearly eager to redeem himself after his hasty misstep. "If that should come to pass, I have a cadre of experienced and loyal men who could 'repair' this situation. Their actions would be untraceable. The act would be blamed on rogue agents of a friendly foreign power. I already have something in mind."

The thought was chilling. A man in the highest political position of the Soviet Union could be eliminated at the whim of a general. The implications were not lost on Romanov. If he was not careful with these kinds of people, he could be destroyed just the same. When it came down to it, power was merely an illusion. All it took was a group of well-trained fanatics to revoke it. Suddenly, he no longer found the rich taste of the cigar so soothing. He dashed it out in the overflowing ashtray.

"Very well, then. Prepare your operatives for such a scenario."

And that was all it took to sentence a man to death.

Kryuchkov stirred in his seat. "We must give the West the idea that we are seeking peace all the while preparing for war. This must be done with the utmost care and precision. Each act must be calculated to give the impression that the Soviet Union is reducing its military presence in Eastern Europe. This will throw NATO off-balance in Europe as its allies will be quick to call for matching this with withdrawals of their own. Let us take meaningless peace initiatives and goodwill gestures that either lulls the West into a false sense of security or tears the alliance apart. When the time comes for war, America and its allies will be stunned by the speed, numbers, and the ferocity of our attack."

Romanov nodded. "Once I am in power then, I will commit to such an action. We will herald a new beginning to our relationship with the West. At the same time, we will conceal the true extent of our build-up near their borders. When the time is right, we will strike. When would be the best time to launch such an attack, Marshall Orgarkov?"

"Late spring. Early summer. No earlier than the first of May. No later than June 1st."

Borisovich spoke up. "What if our force build-up is detected before then?"

All eyes turned to Romanov. It was a dangerous question - one that only a younger man would dare ask. If the Americans presented evidence of what was truly happening, the Soviet Union would face a humiliation greater than the Cuban Missile Crisis. Backing down from such an accusation would be his final act in office. The men here would turn on him to avoid blame. If he were lucky, the rest of Romanov's days would be lived out under house arrest in his dacha near the Crimean Sea. If he were unlucky, his fate would be met at the hands of a firing squad.

Only one answer would suffice for these men, and Romanov gave it.

"We would attack immediately."

AMBUSH

April 2, 1985
Red Square - GUM Department Store rooftop

After sliding the grenade into the launcher tube, Minh sat down and rubbed his palms together. It was freezing and dismal again in Moscow today. How did people live like this? Back in his native land, the sun was almost always shining, and it was warm every day. Simple farmers who had nothing would laugh and sing about the sun while they worked. But here, the icy wind blew all the time. It hollowed out Russian hearts. No one smiled unless it was at the expense of another. This was a cruel place with weather and people to match.

Six months ago, the Russians had brought him here with the utmost secrecy. After countless rehearsals, the day had finally come when he would kill the new general secretary. The intelligence documents they showed him had made the man's intentions clear enough. Mikhail Sergeyevich Gorbachev was secretly negotiating with both China and the West to eliminate Soviet military assistance to the Vietnamese people in exchange for economic favors. Unable to protect itself from its enemies, Minh's homeland would be weak and vulnerable to foreign invasion once again.

Gorbachev's death, the Russians told him, would ensure long-lasting peace and unity in Vietnam. Out in the woods of Siberia, they had made him practice the vulgar act again and again until it was automatic. Each night, a vast outdoor mock-up of Red Square was constructed. To keep the satellites from discovering their real intent, an army of men would take it down just before sunrise. Over six months, Minh's body and mind had been sculpted for this one task. Now finally it would be completed, and he could go back home. He dreamed of the pleasant land and fields every night and ached to return to his mother and father. No more military life for him. The rest of his days would be spent in honest farm labor.

Major Danh tramped across the snowy roof. Minh stifled a laugh at the small frame hidden in the depths of a fur hat and gray overcoat. Even a smile would be impolite. After all, he had lived and trained together with Danh, but they were not friends. The older man's rank and combat experience had marked the major as the head of this operation. Minh was merely a young private. He'd never fired so much as a shot in anger.

"I am told the target is approaching." A dollop of contempt leaked out into Major Danh's words. Minh sensed a dare clinging to the chill air. No, he would never laugh or smile at this man with a scar that ran down his face like a snake.

"The plan." Danh's command was pushed out through numbed syllables.

Minh's brain reeled as he tried to think of how to please the major. Did he want details or just the main thrust? The wind howled and the snow whipped across the flat expanse of the GUM department store's rooftop. Danh gritted his teeth and Minh took it as a sign of impatience.

"Three cars come down this road," Minh spoke. "The middle is the target. Wait for them to reach the intersection. A diversion. Then we attack. Both rockets at the same time." He swept his hand toward the pair of loaded rocket launchers that leaned against the stone railing that ran all along the rooftop.

If Danh was satisfied by Minh's recital, he showed no sign of it. Instead, he reached inside a deep pocket and pulled out the map.

"When it is finished, we go down there and get separate taxis. Go to this address."

Minh peered at the map of central Moscow with a red circle near the frayed edge. In the margins were written the street name and a number. It was directly across the street from the Vietnamese embassy. The sudden change to the plan made Minh's gut twist.

"Are we not to go with Boris?" he asked.

Danh shook his head. "I don't trust these Russians. They took my pistol."

"Why?"

"Exactly."

Minh shivered. It may have been from the cold or his nerves - he could no longer tell. There were no signs of treachery below in Red Square. Across the vast concrete plain, people hurried back and forth in their usual way. In front of Lenin's Mausoleum, the Red Army soldiers marched in tight mechanical formation. The spires of Kazan Cathedral bore mute witness to the lurching progress of daily life in the heart of the Soviet capital.

He ducked his head back down and nodded at Danh. "Everything seems fine."

Somehow the words failed to comfort his superior officer. The major wrestled his hand out from a heavy glove and checked his watch.

"They are late," he announced.

Minh's bowels clenched at the news. He glanced at the rocket launchers and then at Danh.

"Perhaps they're -."

A horn blasted four times in the distance. Danh's eyes went wide, and he lifted the binoculars to his face.

"They are coming. Get ready."

Minh cradled the RPG-18 in his hands like a small child. Three black cars with tinted windows crawled down the narrow roadway. His chest tightened and the dream-like quality of the last six months drifted away in the wind. When the vehicles turned right along Nikolskaya Street, Danh set down the binoculars and picked up his launcher. An engine roared, and tires squealed as two cars pulled up behind the motorcade.

Another pair of vehicles sped down the street in front and swerved at the last minute, leaving no room for the Soviet leader's car to advance. The trap was sprung.

With nowhere else to go, the men in the security detail jumped from the lead vehicle and sprayed long bursts of automatic weapons at the ambushers. The reinforced bullet-proof glass in the ambush cars clinked as the rounds slapped into them.

Minh hefted the rocket launcher on his shoulder and aimed at the car stuck in the middle of the motorcade. Danh raised a hand. The command was clear. Wait. But for what?

The general secretary's bodyguards reloaded while the driver of the lead car pinned the accelerator and gunned the engine. A sick squealing of tires and metal filled the air as he rammed the attacker's car. It was just enough to create a one-meter space between the ambush vehicle and the nearby building. The lead motorcade car squeezed between the narrow gap and the general secretary's car followed. Minh swallowed back the urge to shout at Danh, whose hand stayed up like a flagpole. Couldn't he see their target was escaping?

"Sir...," Minh said. The word slipped out in a soft breath. Danh's hand fell. The spell was broken.

One. Two. Three. Minh squeezed the trigger.

CLICK.

Danh looked back over at him in horror. The launcher dropped from his hands and clattered on the icy rooftop. Needles of fear dug into Minh, and suddenly he felt like a mouse caught in a trap.

Far below in the street, a police car drove straight for the scene. At the last possible moment before collision, the vehicle veered into a tight skid and halted inches from the bumper of the lead vehicle. The general secretary's car stopped as the police car's rear doors opened. Two blue-uniformed men stepped out and reached inside the backseat. Minh watched in confusion as they pulled out a pair of rocket-propelled grenade launchers. In a practiced motion, both of them shouldered the weapons and fired. The grenades made a sound like a hammer on a barrel as they leaped from the launchers.

The general secretary's car left the ground as the explosive rounds tore through the windshield followed by a blood orange flash.

All around the burning vehicle lay sprawled bodies of dead and dying men as the gray pavement turned crimson from the growing pool of blood. One of the police officers ran up to the vehicle with a pistol drawn. His steps were deft and nimble. When he arrived at the stricken limo, he fired two quick shots that rang out all along Red Square. Minh watched the police officers climb back into the boxy police car and speed away from the grisly scene.

From three stories up, the smell of death and burnt tires wafted up into Minh's nostrils.

"But - but!" he heard himself say.

Something terrible had just happened, but the pieces wouldn't fit together in his mind. Hadn't the Russians brought them both here to kill the general secretary? What were the police officers doing down there? None of this made any sense!

Minh felt the sting of a slap to his face as the major screamed at him.

"We've been betrayed!" he shouted. "We need to go. Now!"

The major grabbed him by the sleeve and broke into a run.

"Let's go!" he shouted. "The staircase!"

Minh sensed the urgency in Danh's voice. They were in terrible danger, and they needed to get far away. The only option was to get into the street, find a car, and go wherever Danh told them. The major had suspected things were not right from the start of the operation. He had planned ahead. There was a place where they could hide for a little while and then go home. If there was still a chance he could return home to Vietnam, he would take it.

Each stride across the rooftop made him wish harder. He would pay any price to get away from this dark and unhappy place. After this nightmare was over, there would be no more adventures. He would find a girl and farm for the rest of his days. He tried to remember how the warm sun felt on his skin, but the memory was wiped out by the panic.

Halfway across the roof, the streets below were suddenly filled by an angry chorus of sirens. A battalion of boots thundered against the pavement. These were the sounds of being hunted. Minh clung tight to the fading light of hope that propelled him onward.

Ten steps away from the maintenance door, it swung open and Boris stepped out, a Makarov pistol clutched in his hand.

The dark fur of the KGB handler's cap bristled in the wind. A sick grin creased his face. It held no trace of friendship. No need to carry on the ruse. It was over.

"Halt!" The man's voice was like gravel.

Minh stopped. Danh growled and bolted towards the tall Russian. From out of nowhere, a knife blade flashed in the major's hand. A single shot barked and Danh fell face down in the snow.

Boris swivelled the gun in Minh's direction.

"I always hated him. You - you were not so bad. Any last words before I shoot you like a dog?" he asked.

Minh gazed down from the stone parapet at the chaos in Red Square below. Dozens of soldiers and police streamed towards the GUM entrances like angry ants. He was trapped.

He turned back to Boris and sang the first line of a song his mother would sing to him when he was a child. For an instant, he was back home with his family, standing in the rice fields with his feet planted in the soft mud. A smile creased his father's dirty face. His mother emerged from the thatched hut. One look at Minh and she ran to him.

The wooden bridge is bound with nails,
The bamboo bridge is rough and difficult to cross…

Minh heard the shot. Everything went dark but nothing hurt. Nothing hurt.

OPERATION HALLUCINATION

April 10, 1985
The Kremlin

Each uniformed man at the table was sworn to do whatever was necessary to defend their country.

That time was now upon them.

They were the heads of the Red Army's most essential service branches. In front of them sat tall stacks of official reports about combat readiness. General Secretary Romanov wasn't a fool - he knew some of the documents were about as accurate as a fairy tale. Instead of accepting them at face value, he had loosened the truth from them by having the secretaries pour a generous amount of vodka in their tea glasses. By 3 in the morning, the tea was gone, but the vodka kept flowing - and so did the lies. Now it was dawn, and the office reeked of cigarette smoke, sweat, and half-truths.

Many years ago, a Soviet leader would demand such lies from his generals and receive them in return. The result was often a shocking waste of lives and material. General Secretary of the Communist Party of the Soviet Union Grigory Romanov had seen it himself as a junior officer in The Great Patriotic War. That time was thankfully over. These days, decisions had to be made based on evidence and expert opinion, and that was why they were all gathered here, drunk and tired and ready to talk frankly. The answers these men provided were critical.

If the land forces were not up to the task of destroying capitalism, then it would fall to the rocket forces to do the job. Romanov had hoped to avoid such a destructive war, but over the past several months, he had grown increasingly convinced that a conflict of some sort was inevitable. Preparations had been concealed for months.

Time had run out.

The question in his mind hung like the Sword of Damocles. Was the Red Army ready to wage a worldwide war against the imperialists? If the answer was yes, they would be taking the biggest gamble in history. If no, the world was doomed to bathe in nuclear hellfire.

Romanov inhaled the stale cigarette smoke that lingered in the air. "And so, gentleman - I will ask you for the final time. Are the branches of the Soviet Red Army capable of carrying out this plan?"

Ten lonely ticks of the nineteenth-century clock on his desk marked the silence that split question and answer.

A hand shot up. It was Chief Marshall Tolubko of the artillery forces.

"Comrade general secretary, my men are ready and willing to support this plan. We are confident of the recent reorganization at the battalion level. I beg you, however, to reconsider the use of advanced weaponry to allow for fast breakthroughs along the front," he slurred.

Romanov shuddered. Was the man mad? The other officers stared down at the table. How could he deny this request without making an enemy?

"I understand the short-term advantages that nuclear weapons might confer upon our military forces," he said. "But that would introduce an element of unpredictability in how the West would respond to their use. No, comrade marshall. We must fight this war using the weapons we are most familiar with - tanks and soldiers."

Tolubko flinched as if he had been slapped by a mistress.

Romanov's next words were meant as a balm on the wound. "Your artillery will, of course, play a key role in the war. Without it, our plan would not have a chance of succeeding. We are all counting on you for ultimate victory."

The marshall smiled and sipped at the vodka. "Of course, comrade general secretary. And you will have it."

Romanov felt as if he had narrowly avoided a head-on collision. These men at the table were not used to being commanded by others. They were used to giving the orders and often acted like children when denied something. One bruised ego was dangerous. If Gorbachev's cruel fate had taught him anything, it was that Grigory Romanov could also be replaced.

Marshall of the Air Force Kuldanov spoke next. "The plan will succeed. No question. The air force is ready to do its duty."

Of course, Kuldanov would say that. Since the scandalous shoot-down of a Korean airliner over the Sea of Japan nearly a year and a half ago, he was a man with a black mark on his record. The eager show of support from Kuldanov could only be an attempt to get back in the graces of the Kremlin leadership. Romanov couldn't let it go so easily. Most of the men at the table needed constant praise but this one needed to be beaten down again and again with his own failures.

"That is good to hear," Romanov said. "But the reports I have read show that American technology has allowed their fighter aircraft to leap ahead an entire generation in recent years. Many of our planes are old, and our pilots lack training. What makes you so sure the air force will be prepared to handle this venture?"

Kuldanov's face turned ashen at the rebuke. Romanov felt a trickle of shame for inflicting the humiliation. After all, the marshall was a combat ace and had served in the skies over the Motherland in the last war. Kuldanov dabbed at the sweat on his brow then stammered out a response.

"That is understood at every level. But if we are given the element of surprise, I can assure you that key NATO airfields in West Germany will be put out of action in the first hours of the war. Eventually, NATO's air forces will recover from the blow. By that time, our tanks and men will be at the Rhine."

Romanov weighed the words in his mind. They were filled with the optimism of a man who wanted to retain his job. But on the whole, they matched closely enough to what he had been told about him earlier.

By the end of the war, win or lose, Marshall Kuldanov would command little more than the flaming debris and cratered runways that were once the proud property of the Red Army Air Force. Retirement would come with a pension and a medal instead of a bullet to the brain stem. It was the best Kuldanov could hope for at this point.

General Vasiliev coughed and raised a tentative hand. This man was not a marshall, but he belonged here at the table anyway. As the highest-ranking member of the Signals branch, his opinion would be invaluable. After all, modern warfare was dependent on reliable and speedy communications. Romanov gestured toward the man and listened carefully as he spoke up. Unlike the older men in the room, he was not used to guarding his thoughts.

"Signals is ready, but there are reservations. Jamming on this level has never been attempted before. NATO will attempt to jam our signals too. The effect will be chaotic. I predict that whoever wins this war will be the one who manages to operate in radio silence amid the confusion. On the first day, we will give our officers a destination and tell them to drive straight for it. The men under them will be told, in the absence of orders, to continue going west. Simple but effective."

"Very good," said Romanov. The praise slipped out unintentionally. The marshalls glared at the younger man as he shuffled through his notes. Now he had done it. The dollop of approval had earned Vasiliev new rivals. Romanov wondered if it would goad the other men at the table to work harder. Or perhaps it would be their undoing. Romanov castigated himself. He should have been more careful. Each word he cast out now sent ripples into the dark waters of the future.

Mercifully, a young woman from the outer hallway came in and poured a new pot of tea for each man. The water scalded his tongue, but Romanov kept from flinching, keenly aware of what it meant to show weakness in front of these men.

"Go ahead, comrade," he said to Mikhailov. "I am interested in what you will say."

The general of the armored troops patted the table with one hand and breathed in deep. This was the essential news. Sure, signals, the artillery and air might be ready. But if the bread and butter of the Red Army was not up to the task, then all this was for naught. The plan would die here and now in this room. Nuclear weapons would be the next inevitable resort.

"The troops are ready and willing to carry out their duty to the Motherland. Morale is high. The lack of our tank's technological sophistication is made up for in sheer weight of their numbers. We will suffer losses - sometimes appalling losses. But we must have faith in the ability of the average fighting man to carry on his mission despite these hardships. We saw this out in the last war. Our allies…are not as reliable. But with the right sort of encouragement, they will do their duty. Of that, I know."

Romanov gulped the tea down and set his glass on the table. His cheeks felt suddenly hot, and the world tilted for a long second. The plan would work. Had to work. Seven days to the Rhine River. In a matter of days, they would carry out an operation so daring and so fast that the world would be shocked into submission. Forty years of bitter rivalry would come to its logical conclusion. He lifted an empty glass to the room and smiled.

"Gentlemen, the decision is made then. Continue your preparations. Very soon, we march west."

A NEED FOR SPEED

April 28, 1985
85,000 feet above Central Europe

Captain Noah "Reaper" Stoltz gazed out the SR-71's cockpit at the planet below. From up here, the curvature of the Earth arced across the bottom half of his vision. The soft whites of the cumulus layers were spread out before him in a mirage-like sheen.

Below the clouds lay the carpet of green and gold of Central Europe. Above were the purples and blacks that could only be seen at the edge of space. The stars were countless pinpricks of light that dotted the upper portion of his view. Despite all the hours spent flying the sleek Blackbird reconnaissance plane all over the world, the scenery never failed to impress. It reminded him of just how fragile and alone mankind really was among such calm beauty. In a few seconds, he would be passing east over the Iron Curtain and into dangerous territory, but from up here it all looked so peaceful.

The radio crackled in his ear. Stoltz's gaze returned to the softly lit displays of the instrument panel.

"Got one."

The baritone voice belonged to his Radar Systems Officer, Major Dean Morrissey, callsign "Hammer," who was responsible for navigating the aircraft and operating its cameras and electronic defenses.

For Stoltz, Morrissey was the better half of a smooth-running crew with no less than eight years and thirty classified missions under their belt.

Stoltz waited and said nothing. Soon enough, the RSO would tell him what he needed to know. There was an unwritten rule between them that no one rushed the other. After a puff of silence, Stoltz's headset clicked again, and Morrissey spoke in a serene tone.

"SAM launch. Bearing oh-six-two. Distance two five."

The Blackbird's Threat Warning Receiver chirped, confirming Morrissey's announcement. The enemy surface-to-air missile was out there to the east - snaking upwards and straining to meet the plane's trajectory and altitude.

The SR-71 could not out-turn it. Just cornering the aircraft at this speed would take nearly a hundred miles. Unlike the small nimble fighter aircraft that could jink their way around such problems, the Blackbird was not built for such quick maneuvering. It was made for another purpose entirely.

Pure. Raw. Speed.

Stoltz nudged the throttle forward and turned off the ECM jammer. A small shudder flowed through the plane as the twin Pratt and Whitney engines flared. The MACH indicator's needle climbed past Mach 3. With its target traveling at more than three times the speed of sound, the incoming missile would struggle to maintain the aircraft in its forward targeting envelope. To do so would require trading altitude for velocity, neither of which it could afford on its already tight budget of energy and fuel.

The TWR chirped again. Morrissey's voice slid into his ear.

"Two more launches."

Stoltz listened as the bearing and distance were read out to him. It was nice to know, but there was nothing left to do but keep flying straight. These sites were well over fifty kilometers away, and the missiles had zero chance of getting near him. He chuckled and keyed the intercom.

"Just some SAM battery commander putting on a show," he said. "Good luck down there, buddy."

Morrissey didn't say anything. The busy clicks and taps behind Stoltz were enough to end the conversation there.

Far below, the dark forests and snaking rivers of Eastern Europe swept towards them. Just beyond was the Soviet Union itself.

Stoltz shifted his attention to the clock. Within two minutes, they would be over the target and taking high-resolution photos of three new Soviet military command installations and an airbase that weren't supposed to be there. The DIA handler who briefed them had insisted the Soviets were playing a rigged shell game with their ground units, announcing their disbandment when really they were being sent west for a possible invasion. It all sounded a bit far-fetched, but Stoltz had been sent out on missions on much slimmer pretexts.

He turned his attention to the timer and focused on the flight plan as the world rolled by underneath him. Soon, they would take the photos and then he would turn north towards Scandinavia. After that, it was a dogleg west to RAF Mildenhall where Detachment 4 of 9th Strategic Reconnaissance Wing was based. In less than an hour from now, he would be in the officer's mess hall, eating lunch.

"Hey, I got something," said Morrissey. "Bogeys." It came out like a question and held none of the usual confident assurance.

Stoltz waited to hear the RSO's report. No doubt the Russians were scrambling fighters to come and get him. Since they had upgraded their radar systems in the last two years, such intercepts had become much more frequent. But even when they managed to detect the Blackbird's intrusion on their airspace, it was already too late. By the time the MiGs were in the air, the Blackbird was long gone.

"Foxbat?" It was the NATO designation for the MiG-25, a high-speed aircraft built specifically to intercept American jets. They were indeed fast but not invincible. Stoltz had dealt with the planes several times while flying over Soviet airspace. Not one of them had managed to do much more than track him for a few brief seconds.

The RSO groaned. "Hang on."

Warsaw zoomed past on the left before the RSO spoke again.

"Three - make that four hostiles inbound. Vectoring straight towards us. Range one hundred miles. Bearing zero zero three. Angels seventy-two."

Stoltz's neck crawled with sweat. "Seventy-Two?" he asked.

"Affirm. Seventy-two thousand feet. Now climbing."

It was well-known within the Blackbird community that armed Foxbats would never be able to reach beyond 68,000 feet. Either these MiG-25s were just coming up to say hello or...Stoltz took a deep breath.

"Foxhounds," he said.

The MiG-31 Foxhound was still somewhat of a dark horse among Blackbird crews, but he had been briefed on what little information could be gathered by NATO intelligence. The gist of it was that these planes were faster, better-armed, and more technologically advanced than the Foxbat. As such, they posed a much more serious threat to the Blackbird than the older plane. Approaching head-on at closing speeds greater than Mach 5, the enemy planes would be upon them any second. A decision needed to be made soon.

"Closing fast here," said Morrissey. "You want to start a turn?"

"You got your pictures yet?" asked Stoltz.

"Ten more seconds."

Stoltz's Nomex-gloved hand gripped the flight stick. "Get your pictures and we're out of here."

In his head, he counted down from ten to zero. The pressure suit wrapped around his body suddenly felt constricting. Each warm humid breath swept against the front of his helmet's face shield. When he was halfway finished his countdown, the threat receiver whistled twice. The Foxhounds had locked him up and were about to fire. His heart sank.

"Time's up," he announced.

"Almost...there."

A shrill electronic bell whooped at Stoltz. It could mean only one thing. The enemy planes had locked him up. He knew he should start the turn but doing so might ruin the photos. The mission would need to be flown again, and though his superior officers would reassure him it was okay, a little black mark would go into his file somewhere. Someone else would have to come up here and risk their neck at the whim of a guy in the DIA who "had a hunch."

He kept the plane steady. Somewhere out there, an enemy aircraft was about to shoot at him. It was now or never. He waited a heartbeat and gently pulled the flight stick left. The world outside his cockpit gently tilted.

"Missile launch!" shouted Morrissey.

Stoltz fought the urge to bank the plane harder. Doing so at this speed would stress the aircraft beyond its breaking point and send it into an uncontrollable roll or a flat spin. He squeezed his leg muscles. In the backseat, the RSO was running the array of countermeasures in the plane's DEF systems. All there was left to do for the pilot was to fly the plane and pray the missile didn't hit. The only comfort was the fact that the enemy wouldn't get a second chance at the interception. If the missile was evaded, they'd be home free. Otherwise - well, he didn't really have to worry about that, did he?

Up ahead, the southern coastline of Scandinavia beckoned him. He tried not to picture the missile streaking towards his plane. The oxygen that poured up into his helmet served to calm him. Two deep breaths were all it took to bring his heart rate back to normal. By the end of the second breath, the ringing in his ears halted.

"Missile clear."

"You get the pictures?"

"Yup."

And with that one simple word, they were saved.

Stoltz suddenly remembered today's lunch menu at Mildenhall. It was Tuesday, which meant turkey sandwiches.

After this morning, they would taste extra good.

MORNING IN AMERICA

April 30, 1985
The Oval Office
Washington, D.C.

Keith Tracton barged into the president's office with his leather document case tucked under his arm. Gone was the old manila folder he used to tote around everywhere. The 1980s were in full swing now, and the American economy was soaring. After emerging from a rocky recession, the decade had finally found its rhythm. People were making money and showing off by spending it. Appearances mattered now. So did national security.

"Mister President, I'm sorry to disturb you" he said. "But we found something irregular that needs your immediate attention."

Heath swept into the room hot on his heels. "Irregular?" he said. "Understatement of the decade. We caught them red-handed!"

Reagan stood up and gestured toward the Secret Service agent who loomed in the doorway. Tracton couldn't help but think about all the extra layers of security wrapped around the man that weren't there four years ago. The near-fatal shooting of the president had prompted a massive shift in attitude toward security measures. In fact, it seemed like everything had changed since 1980.

The West had recovered from the stumbles of the 1970s and now had a renewed sense of purpose and optimism. Communism was in retreat everywhere thanks to an aggressive foreign policy and a build-up of conventional forces that the world hadn't seen since the Second World War. It really seemed, as Reagan had proclaimed in his re-election ads, "morning in America."

"Now hold on a moment," said the president. "Let's slow down here. I'm an old man, remember." The wry smile spread across his face as he rounded the desk and extended a hand.

Tracton shook it but not too hard. The president's grip was no longer as firm as it had been before the shooting. In fact, the man's health was much worse than had been reported in the press. Rumors were floating around that his mental acuity had dulled with occasional lapses in memory. In the last six months, a protective circle had formed around Reagan, and no one who gossiped at length about these issues was ever allowed access to the president again. There were some things you just didn't talk about in Washington, D.C. and this was one of them.

"Mr. President, we have some alarming news about the Soviets," said Heath. "We are in big trouble."

Tracton sat down while the new CIA director gave the impromptu briefing. Heath had been promoted to the position after the previous director resigned due to health-related issues. Now at the very pinnacle of a long career, he had taken to the new job with relish. In 1985, the agency had its hands full in every corner of the globe. Though Tracton was satisfied with his position at NSA, he couldn't help feel a trace of jealousy.

"The imaging systems on our planes were upgraded recently. New software," said Heath. "Our cameras can basically see down right through certain objects like clouds and treetops. A few days ago, we got some pictures back that show the Russians are up to no good."

He jerked a thumb at Tracton. "Tell him, Keith."

Tracton set down his coffee and pulled out the photographs from his case. He laid the first shot carefully in front of Reagan and patted the glossy surface.

"This one shows a large wooded area in Thuringia," he said. "It's an East German state right near the border with West Germany. As you can see, there appears to be nothing special about this area. It's beech forest mixed with ash and maple trees. A huge canopy of trees that extend for nearly 75 square kilometers. One of the biggest forest in central Europe. Tell me, Mister President. What do you see except for the tops of the trees?"

Reagan picked up the photograph and shrugged. "Maybe my eyes are too old, but I don't see anything."

Heath jumped in. "Exactly! Show him the next one."

Tracton had the edge of the photo paper between his fingers when the phone rang. Reagan sighed and used the arm of the couch for support to stand. While the ringing filled the room, the president ambled towards his desk and picked up the receiver. He nearly spoke into the wrong end before correcting himself.

Heath and Tracton exchanged glances. That was new.

Both men made small talk and pretended not to listen to the exchange, but it was obvious that Reagan was talking about an upcoming trip to Germany. The itinerary had included a ceremonial visit to Bitburg to visit a cemetery where members of the SS were interred. The president's critics were vocal and angry about it, even though no one had intended to honor the war criminals.

Reagan's voice shot out through the room with a biting tone. No trace of his trademark folksy California tone was detectable.

"You tell the press that I'm going there, anyway…Yes, I understand people are concerned. There are Americans buried there too. What we need now is healing between our nations."

Reagan hung up and marched back to the sofa. His eyes were no longer glassy and far away. He looked straight at Heath and Tracton and leaned forward.

"You gentlemen have come here to brief me on a grave matter. Let's hear it," he said.

Straight and to the point. It was the old Reagan back again and in a fighting mood. That was a very good thing considering what was about to happen.

Tracton pulled the next photo out and laid it beside the first. Instead of the dark tree cover of the Thuringian forest, the frame was filled with the clear outlines of Russian tanks and armored vehicles. Hundreds and hundreds of them. To make his point, Tracton revealed the third photograph, this one zoomed in on several of the vehicles. Their shape was unmistakably that of armored combat vehicles.

"This is the same area of land as shown in the first photo," said Tracton. "This picture shows the 8th Guards Army in advance positions. At first, we couldn't figure out how they were getting all that hardware there without detection, but it appears the East Germans have dug an extensive network of underground tunnels from nearby highways and train stations. These dark spots indicate the entrances and exits. The government announced a massive public works projects in late December. They've had months to build it."

Heath spoke up. "Sir, both our agencies worked on this operation together. What we found were sites like this all along the border with West Germany. The Red Army is in position and ready to pounce at any minute."

Tracton wasn't sure how Reagan would take the news. Nixon had laughed off his warning about the Yom Kippur War back in 1973. Carter wouldn't listen to Heath about the Iranians in early '79.

Reagan brought the photos up to his face. "You say they're preparing for war? Are you sure about this?"

Heath and Tracton nodded in unison. "Positive."

"I'm about to go into a meeting with the Joint Chiefs. Have they been briefed?"

"Yes, sir," said Heath. "They want more information."

Reagan's eyes narrowed. "What else do you have?"

"A very reliable warning," said Heath. "We have good intel from a high-ranking double agent. Something is about to happen. Within the next week to ten days."

Tracton knew all about the agency's most valuable asset, a disillusioned KGB colonel named Oleg Gordievsky. For years, he had given MI6 a treasure trove of solid information about what was really happening in the Kremlin. Stationed in London at the Soviet embassy, he had stumbled upon a cable to destroy all documents before May 2nd and prepare to return home. The alarm bells went off when another memo from the KGB directorate requesting specific details of Reagan's upcoming visit to Europe and the security arrangements that were being made.

Reagan cleared his throat. "Well, it looks like my trip to Germany is canceled."

Tracton smiled, relieved to hear the news.

"Good idea," he said in unison with Heath.

If the Soviets launched an offensive with the American president in Europe, the results would be a chaotic mess. Calling the shots from across an ocean would be nearly impossible. If Reagan were killed in an attack, it would have added fuel to the nightmare.

Sure, the line of succession was spelled out clearly enough back in the 18th century. In practice, though, it had been less than smooth. One need only have looked at the issues surrounding who was in charge when Reagan had been shot back in 1981. Tracton remembered the in-fighting that had resulted when Alexander Haig had wrongly informed the press, "I'm in control here."

Both intelligence men laid the final card on the table. If this didn't get things moving, Tracton had no idea what would work.

"Our friends in Afghanistan captured an elite Soviet paratrooper four days ago," said Heath. "Under advanced interrogation, he confessed to being part of a plot to kill Gorbachev earlier this month. When he was passed over to our agents, he gave out names and details that only someone directly involved in the assassination would know. All of it checked out."

Reagan's face grew dark. He shook his head and looked out the window. The afternoon sunlight filtered in, blanketing the room with its golden radiance.

"It's a lot to take in," he said. "I had faith that Gorbachev would work together with us to move the world closer to peace. I should have known something was seriously wrong. The system they've built over there…it kills anyone who defies its brutal logic."

Tracton spoke up. "We all wanted to believe it, sir. When the Soviet hardliners announced they would continue the work that Gorbachev started, it seemed too good to be true.

Looking at these pictures, we now have proof it was exactly that."

The president took a deep breath and nodded. He stood up, which was the signal that the meeting was now over.

"Gentlemen, what you've presented here is evidence of a direct threat to the United States and its allies. Given your assessment of the situation, I have no choice but to act in the face of this aggression. Once I consult with the joint chiefs on this matter, I'll make a decision about raising the alert level. I'll also need to get Peggy to write something up for tonight's speech."

Tracton and Heath walked out of the room together. None of them dared say a word to each other until they were in the back of the agency vehicle. Swept religiously for bugs, the sedan was among the most secure places in Washington to freely discuss the dangers to the nation.

"You called it," said Tracton. "Four or five years. Happy now?"

"Somehow 'I told you so' doesn't seem so satisfying to say right now."

The driver pulled onto the beltway. The afternoon traffic was light, but soon it would be clogged with government workers commuting back home to Maryland. Tracton watched the driver beside them pull past doing sixty and shook his head, trying hard not to think about it all going up in flames.

"Man, I wish I was one of them," said Heath. "Just some poor schmuck oblivious to what's about to happen. Ignorance is bliss. That's damn right."

"You ever think that maybe we pushed them to it? I mean - the last few years...we shoved back hard. Maybe too hard."

"What?! No. It's like you said. The wheels were coming off their system. This is their fault. They knew the car was a lemon, but they kept driving it anyway. Come on, Keith."

Tracton rubbed his temples, replaying the key events of the world he had helped form these past few years. Missile defense. Military build-ups. A six-hundred-ship navy. Intermediate missiles. At the time, everyone was convinced it was defensive. It seemed so obvious that no one had questioned it.

"If it comes - if it really happens, what do you think will be the motivation will be?" he asked.

"Same reason wars always happen. Ignorance. Greed. Fear -."

Tracton pointed a finger as the last word came out. "Exactly. Fear. We put so much attention on pushing them back at every turn. Just consider for a moment they got the wrong message. What did we do to assure them? I'm not talking about speeches. I'm referring to real concrete steps to de-escalate things."

"I'll admit you might be right," Heath answered. "But what can we really do about any of it at this stage?"

To that question, Tracton had no answer. The car drove on and both men carried on with their day, doing their best to shut the implications of the meeting out of their mind.

Eight hours later, Reagan warned the Soviets in a televised address to the nation and raised the alert level to DEFCON 2.

Six hours after that, the world was at war.

DEADLINES AND DOOMSDAYS

CBS NEWS SPECIAL REPORT TRANSCRIPT
New Series Volume 11
No. 12
May, 1985

Invasion of West Germany (Bulletin 1-1)

ANNOUNCER: From CBS News headquarters in New York, here is Dan Rather.

DAN RATHER: Good Monday morning. Reports that the Soviet Union and its allies have invaded West Germany have been confirmed. Pentagon spokesman Frank Hoffman said in a White House press briefing early this morning that quote 'the Warsaw Pact has been conducting large-scale conventional military operations against NATO allies in Western Europe since earlier today' unquote. Hoffman also stated that President Reagan would address the nation in a broadcast speech before nine A.M. central time. That's twenty-five minutes from now.

Standing by at the White House is CBS correspondent Rob Plante. Rob, I understand the briefing has just concluded. What else did Hoffman say?

ROB PLANTE: Dan, they told us that the president has been moved to a secure location and has ordered all US forces around the globe to their highest security level.

There were no specific mentions of how the fighting was going at this point but Hoffman confirmed that American forces in West Germany were currently engaged along the inner German border. As of two hours ago, reservists throughout the United States were ordered to active duty and told to report to their units. Hoffman also mentioned that the administration has called for an emergency meeting at the United Nations to call a halt to the hostilities. The Soviets have yet to respond to the request but the UN has said they're going ahead with the meeting regardless.

Another interesting point is that the conflict seems to be spreading. The Pentagon spokesman reported clashes along the North and South Korean border. He also mentioned there had been naval clashes between Soviet and American ships in the Straits of Hormuz. For obvious reason, he could not elaborate on specific details. When one reporter asked point blank whether the United States was at war with the Soviet Union, Hoffman told him quote 'that appears to be the case at the present time' unquote.

RATHER: Rob, I want to be sure that I understand the situation and that our viewers do too. The United States is officially at war with the Soviets right now?

PLANTE: That is what we were told in the briefing, Dan. As you know, there were stories coming out of West Germany last night that several major NATO airfields had been attacked by what appeared to be saboteurs or terrorist groups. Two American generals, one in Italy and the other in Germany, were killed by what appeared to be car bombs planted on their personal vehicles. Civilians living near military installations reported hearing and seeing explosions and gunfire. The West German government issued an emergency alert and called up their reservists about an hour before we did. Towns and cities near the border have been ordered to evacuate but it's not clear how many people managed to get out before the fighting started.

RATHER: Any reports of nuclear weapons being used so far?

PLANTE: No. Hoffman denied that any nuclear weapons had been used or launched. There were rumors swirling around early on that something had happened. European news agencies reported widespread broadcast interference just before dawn.

Many of them suddenly went off the air, sparking panic that they were destroyed in a nuclear attack. However, it appears that the stations were attacked by some kind of electronic jamming. A few of them have returned to the airwaves despite that and their - and our correspondents in major European cities have been checking in that they are safe. So at this time, whatever's happening over there appears to be limited to a conventional conflict. Hoffman read out a brief statement from the president, appealing for the public to remain calm and optimistic. Again, just to make sure everyone understands at home - there are no reports of nuclear weapons being used.

RATHER: What's going on here, Rob?

PLANTE: Well, obviously the situation is still very unclear at this point, Dan. Military officials are working hard to respond to whatever's happening over there while the experts piece together how and why it happened. As you know, President Reagan spoke to the nation last night, accusing the Soviets of a secret military build-up near the border with West Germany. He also warned them against any kind of attack and raised the alert level to DEFCON TWO.

Right now, the president is trying to appear on top of the situation while working with other leaders to defuse the conflict. Public officials are being careful with the information they are releasing to the public at this time, obviously trying to keep a lid on any widespread panic. The president is due to come on the air in about twenty minutes' time and he's likely to give a more complete picture of the events unfolding. Officials in several government departments have repeated the president's call for calm and have urged people to stay in their homes as the crisis unfolds.

RATHER: Thank you Rob Plante at the White House. Larry McFarlane is in West Germany right now and he's reporting by satellite telephone from Hannover. Larry, if you can hear me - what is the situation over there at the moment?

MCFARLANE: (buzz of static) -here, Dan. There's no question that...happening as I look out the window to the east...explosions and artillery...huge clouds of smoke billowing up over the battlefield...what must be hundreds of tanks and troop carriers coming straight towards us...

RATHER: Larry, we're having a hard time hearing you due to some interference but if I can make out what you're saying, there's some kind of fighting taking place near Hannover. I certainly hope you're safe there and if not, I urge you to leave immediately. What's the situation in the city itself?

MCFARLANE: …chaos over here, Dan…must be thousands of people trapped on the autobahn out to the west. I can see long lines of cars…stuck for miles. There have been (garbled) accidents on the highway. A while back, a pair of helicopters flew straight over and strafed the civilian and military convoys. People inside the city… staying home. Most stores are completely empty and I can't see a single civilian on the street…a while ago about a hundred German reservists showed up and started building barricades down major roads. It seems like everyone here is getting ready to either hunker down or fight.

RATHER: Thank you for that report, Larry. Once again, please leave if the situation is too dangerous. Just one more question, have you talked with anyone in charge over there? Any sense of how things are going for NATO in that area?

MCFARLANE: …a total blackout on any press information. There's - hold on, one moment, Dan. Someone's knocking on my hotel door. (voices in German in the background). Dan, I'm being told by the German militia to leave immediately. Russian tanks are on their way into the city. There's already - there's already some artillery landing to the east of here. I can hear jet engines coming this way too. I need (loud static hissing and then silence).

RATHER: Larry, are you there? Larry, if you can hear me, I want you to get out of there immediately for your own safety. Have we lost him? Okay. (long pause) We'll be back after these commercial messages. President Reagan is set to speak in a few more minutes. Stay tuned.

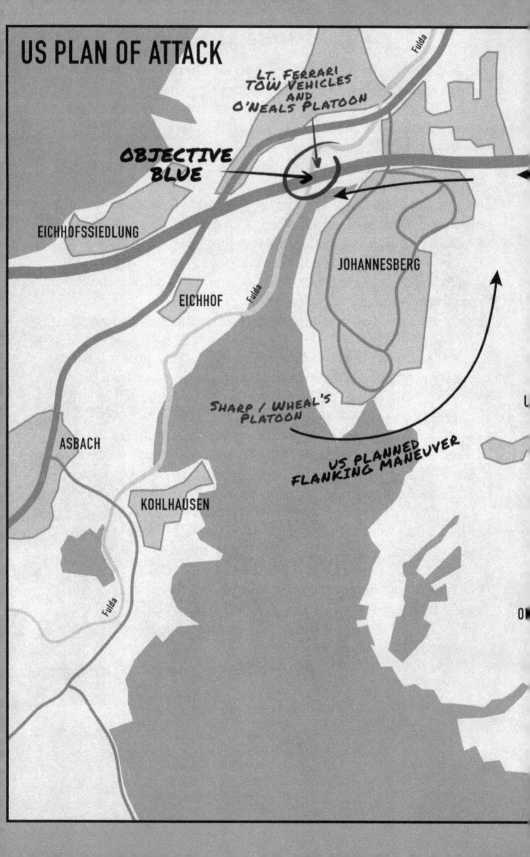

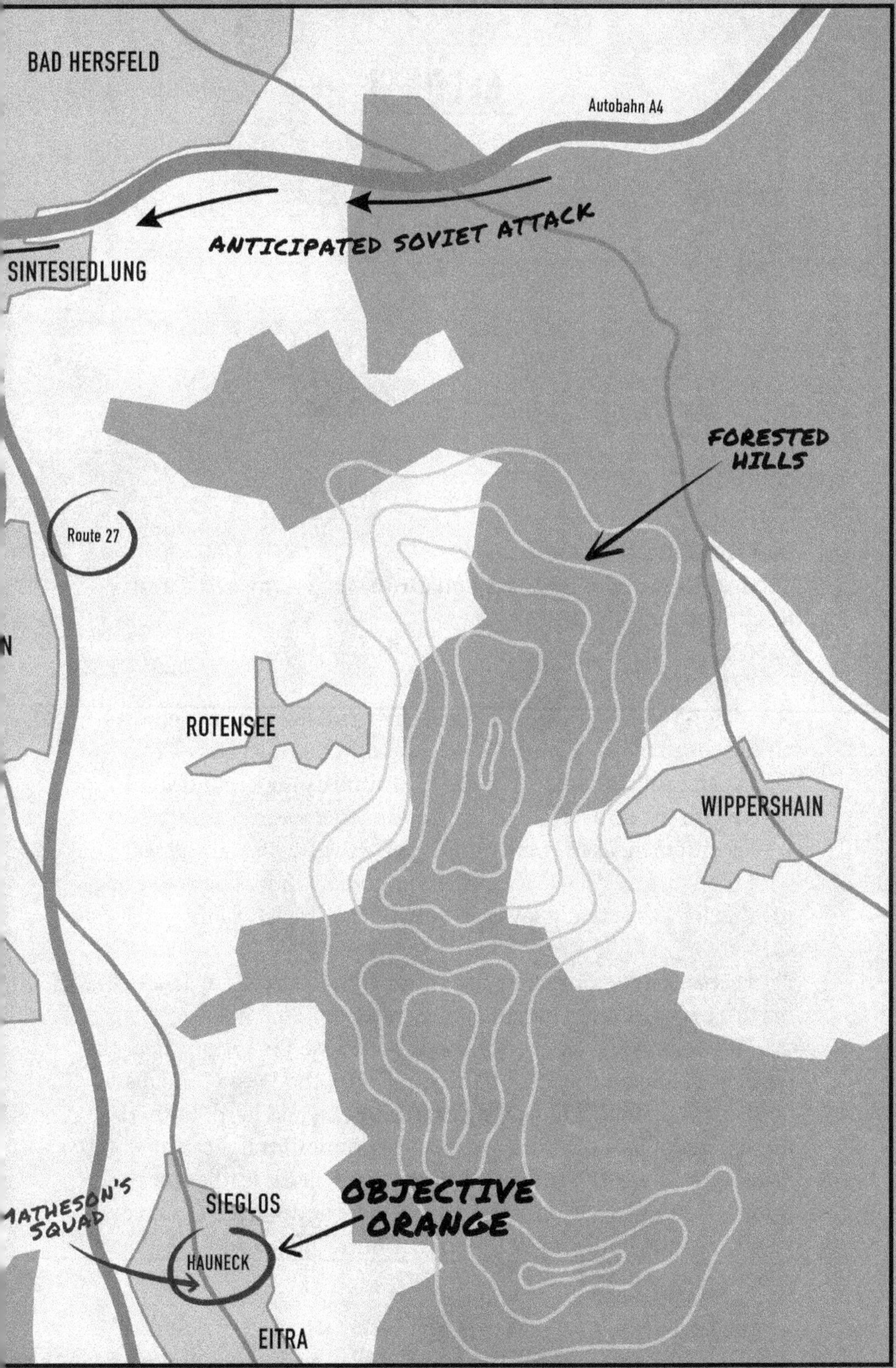
BAD HERSFELD
Autobahn A4
ANTICIPATED SOVIET ATTACK
SINTESIEDLUNG
FORESTED HILLS
Route 27
ROTENSEE
WIPPERSHAIN
SIEGLOS
OBJECTIVE ORANGE
HAUNECK
EITRA

ALLONS!

Bad Hersfeld, West Germany
Tactical Command Post, 1st Squadron, 11th Armored Cavalry
Regiment
0550

Major Todd Schnauffer laid out the wrinkled ink-stained map on the cheap plastic card table and smoothed it with both hands. The small group of officers crowded around as the ground shuddered with the impact of artillery rounds to the east.

"Gentlemen, as of twenty minutes ago, we're officially at war with the Warsaw Pact," Schnauffer announced. It was hard to imagine that he was actually saying those words. The whole thing felt surreal.

He paused for a moment and scanned the dark stony faces of his three troop commanders as the words sunk in.

"Intel says we've got heavy contact at Phase Line Alpha near the border. 2nd Squadron is up there along with the West Germans. Soon enough, they'll be pulling back here fast and hard. In this sector, the major axis of attack seems to be coming straight west along Autobahn Route 4. The Russians are going hell for leather for the bridges. I know we've only just arrived here and started to deploy. If your men aren't dug in yet, they better hurry up because we'll have contact soon enough.

We need to delay those river crossings for as long as possible."

As part of the 11th Armored Cavalry Regiment (the "Black-horse Regiment"), this was the nightmare scenario they had been trained for. Schnauffer squeezed his hand as the adrenaline flooded his body.

Captain Doug Miller's hand shot up. Schnauffer nodded towards the commander of Bandit Troop.

"Look, Miller," he said. "I'm glad you're asking questions but the hand thing's gotta stop. This isn't a math class. We're at war now."

The young captain folded his arms. "Sir, what's our estimate of enemy strength and speed at this point?"

Schnauffer cracked his knuckles and tossed out the bad news like yesterday's trash. "At least two Soviet divisions are heading this way. Latest reports show they're nearly finished with Phase Line Alpha and moving fast towards Baker. Whatever's left of our guys will pull back to Phase Line Concord. After that, they'll be here at our doorstep. This is the last line of resistance. If the Russians find a way over the Fulda River before V Corps is in position, we might just lose the whole damn war."

Captain Kevin Sharp, the leader of Charlie Troop, pointed to the map. "If Ivan's coming down Route 4, that puts them right in the path of my men. Any estimates of what we'll be facing?" The words came out slurred, his Australian accent thick with fatigue.

Schnauffer held back a grin. It was a point of pride that he had a guy initially from Down Under in the squadron. There were plenty of other men from other countries serving in the US Army - but few were from the other side of the planet. It was something to brag about whenever he met another officer in Europe. At the very least, it always earned him a free drink whenever he played the familiar game of "one-upmanship" that officers started playing after a few rounds were imbibed.

"Captain Sharp, I hear that Australians are basically surrounded by creatures that are capable of killing them in countless horrific ways. Let me put it this way - you're about to feel right at home. Prepare for tank-heavy regiments to come and say hello very soon."

Schnauffer rubbed his hands together in the predawn chill. A helicopter's rotor slapped at the air somewhere close by. The squadron commander looked up at the wall of combat netting above and held his breath just before the Cobra sped off.

Satisfied that he was not about to get roasted by a Hind's rockets, the squadron commander spoke again.

"I know your men are already deployed as per last night's orders. There's a small change in the plan though. Sharp, you're primary is still to hold the bridge near Eichhofsiedlung. I also need you to try and hold this little town here too for as long as you can. Hauneck. If the Russians capture it, they'll reroute south and come west around these hills. They'll just bypass the whole area. I wouldn't put it past them to send another force to try for the smaller bridges south of there near Kohlhausen. Captain Miller - that will be your area of responsibility. Keep the Soviets on the eastern side of the river for as long as you can."

Sharp dug into his pocket and pulled out his notebook, jotting down information between brief glances at the topographical map. The major gestured to his S-2, who ran over and slapped a bundle of freshly-typed paper on the plastic card table. Each of the troop commanders grabbed a copy.

"Destroy that as soon as you're done reading it," said Schnauffer. "It's our scheme of maneuver. When I give the signal, pull back west over the bridges. Our engineers will blow them sky high. Make sure you don't hit any friendlies. Radio call signs are the same ones we're using now, but I want everyone silent until we're in contact. Even then, keep your reports short and to the point. We have to assume the radio net's been compromised. It's also guaranteed that the Soviets have direction-finding equipment deployed. Talk costs lives. Use smoke and flares when practical."

The troop commanders flipped through the pages, squinting in the dim light provided by the command post's single shrouded bulb. Schnauffer indulged their curiosity for a few seconds then made a show of checking his watch.

"Unless there are questions, you need to get back to your men now," he said. "Your jeeps are waiting outside. Good luck."

As the junior officers walked away, Schnauffer tapped Sharp's shoulder. The young captain halted mid-stride and turned.

The lines of strain were already showing on his face, and the squadron commander suspected that they would not disappear for a long time. "Sharp, I need to talk to you."

"Sir." The word shot out like an uncoiled spring. Of all the men here, this was the one the major counted on the most right now. And even though he felt confident that Sharp was the right one to do the job, Schnauffer couldn't help but feel he was sacrificing him. The frontage he was asking his troops to defend was too extensive for their force size.

Both of them knew it. And yet, Sharp hadn't said a word. Somehow that only made it worse. Schnauffer took in a deep breath and searched for something to say. Finally, the words spilled out.

"Good luck out there, Sharp. Keep your head out there and do your job. Things will work out."

Without waiting for a response, the major turned and walked away. The time for talk was over.

CAN'T YOU HEAR THAT THUNDER?

Captain Sharp stood in the cupola of his M1 Abrams and slurped from a tin cup. Each swig of thick grainy sludge that resembled coffee made him want to retch. In any other situation, he would have tossed it on the ground and forgotten about it. But now he needed the edge to beat out the fatigue. It nestled in his joints and dulled his thinking. It was as deadly as a Soviet tank and could kill him just the same. If he were to face combat, he needed every weapon at his disposal to push through the ragged exhaustion that smothered his thoughts.

He knew the rest of the men in his troop felt the same and had encouraged them to rest in shifts. The men of Charlie Troop had not even fought their first battle of the war yet, but they were all beyond tired. The enemy wasn't to blame for it. That "favor" was bestowed upon them by the US Army itself.

Along with the rest of 1st Squadron, Charlie Troop had spent the last twelve hours getting shuffled around Fulda like a pack of Vegas playing cards. At first, it had been deployed within a hair's breadth of the border along with the rest of the 11th Armored Cavalry Regiment. Then without warning, the entire squadron had been yanked back on its leash toward its headquarters at Downs Barracks in Fulda. Early this morning, Charlie Troop swapped out one of its infantry platoons with a tank platoon from the squadron's armor company and headed twenty kilometers north.

Upon arriving here, he had followed orders and arranged for his three platoons and support vehicles to dig in around the town of Eichhofsiedlung, a small suburb southwest of the Bad Hersfeld. The wide bridge to the southwest of the city spanned the Fulda River, making it a natural objective for any Soviet forces coming this way. Even with two tank platoons and a scout platoon, defending the bridge would not be an easy task. It was a sure bet the Americans would be outnumbered and outgunned by a much larger Soviet force with follow-on echelons that would rush at them again and again. The original plan was to set one platoon of tanks near the bridge to defend while the other platoon maneuvered around the flank of the oncoming enemy and destroy the aggressors at range while on the move.

Now things had gotten even harder for Sharp and his men. Major Schnauffer's briefing had upped the ante. Charlie Troop would not only need to hold the bridge at Eichhofsiedlung ("Objective Blue"). It would also have to keep the Soviets out of a small town called Hauneck ("Objective Orange") to the south of Bad Hersfeld. Failing to do so would endanger Bravo Troop to the south as it fended off elements of the 79th Guards Tank Division.

It wasn't the sudden alteration in his mission that bothered Sharp. In fact, rapid changes were typical for a US Army cavalry regiment. The officers and men had gotten used to "shifting on the fly" in response to a variety of threats. With a nearly forty-year legacy of monitoring the intra-German border for Soviet invasion, modern cavalry regiments were trained for flexibility, lightning response, and initiative. Consequently, they had their own unique world within the US Army. They were trained and organized a little different, and they had their own terms and language that was distinct from the regular Army units.

Instead of battalions, cavalry regiments were organized into three squadrons. The backbone of each squadron was its three scout "troops", similar in size to a company. A tank company was included in the squadron to augment the squadron's firepower. There were also support troops like logistics and artillery and, like the tank company, these could be mixed and matched with the scout troops to help where needed. As a result, cavalry regiments were small but self-contained fighting units that packed a deadly punch.

Despite their strength and flexibility, the cavalry regiments weren't expected to fend off the Soviets single-handedly like Rambo taking on the National Guard. Nor were they expected to make a stand and get wiped out. Instead, they were to get near the intra-German border in the event of a war and force the oncoming Soviets to deploy their forces for combat, thereby slowing their advance. If the cavalry units did their job right, the heavier NATO combat units would have enough time to mobilize and join the fight.

But even with all the training and structure that worked in Sharp's favor, the fact remained that he didn't have enough manpower to do what had been asked of him. Soon, an entire enemy division would be on its way here, and Charlie Troop would have to keep the Soviets at bay with nothing but eight tanks and thirty scouts. Sure, he also had a couple of TOW jeeps and an M901 TOW launcher to sting the Soviets from long range. But that still wasn't enough to balance it out. Nowhere near enough.

From where his tank was parked at the edge of the woods on a massive hill, he had a sweeping view of the area south of Bad Hersfeld. The valley floor extended three kilometers east. Running north and south along it was Highway 27. The crumbling single lane asphalt slithered through the little towns that spanned the distance between where he stood and the next large hill to the east. Hauneck was less a town than a smattering of tiny burgs that had been conglomerated for the sake of political administration. Two days ago, he would have driven through here without even checking the name of the place. Now it dominated his thoughts. Would the Russians try for it?

To the north of his position was Bad Hersfeld. Most of its 30,000 inhabitants had been evacuated west. Scattered squads of German Territorials had mobilized in the last hour and were busy setting up ambushes and planting mines along the major routes into the city. From Sharp's briefing, it seemed the Soviets were bypassing the larger towns completely and were unlikely to get tangled up in a fight for the city. The Russians wanted to get west as fast as possible and coming straight along the autobahn seemed to be the only way to do that.

Route 4 shot straight east to west across low even ground that passed just to the south of Bad Hersfeld. For any enemy commander in a hurry, it may as well have been a welcome mat. The road was wide and modern and had four lanes divided by a sliver of concrete. It seemed apparent the Russians would come straight down the road. What possible reason would they have to go for Hauneck when the highway beckoned? He loathed changing plans again to account for something that would never happen and made no real sense. He sighed as he looked at the map. Just to please Schnauffer, he would pull a handful of his infantry to go and set up shop in one of the little towns to the south. The token effort would no doubt be noted in the after-action report.

The grumble of a diesel engine made him turn. Standing in the cupola of an M113 was his executive officer, First Lieutenant Ralph Ferrari.

"What's the word?" he asked.

"We need to cover Hauneck too," Sharp muttered.

The XO's eyes narrowed. "Huh? I get the bridge, but we don't have enough to cover the town too."

Sharp drummed on the metal deck of the M1 and shrugged. "Orders."

"No help?"

Sharp shook his head. "We're spread like Vegemite on toast here."

"I don't know what the hell Vegemite is, but it doesn't sound good."

"Yeah."

"You want to pull a couple of guys out to cover the town for a bit? It's enough to say we tried."

Sharp took a thimble of comfort from the fact that his XO had the same idea. They couldn't possibly hold both objectives at the same time.

"Hang on and let me think about this," he answered.

Ferrari ran a hand over his five o'clock shadow and waited. Sharp considered the large hill with the long gentle slope that faced

east into the valley near Hauneck. Across from it lay another forested hill that would provide perfect cover for an advancing enemy
force. The thought of Soviet tanks charging over a wooded hillside
and going all-out for Orange nearly made him laugh.

"You know what? Tell Sergeant Matheson to mount up with a
couple of infantry squads and get down south," Sharp pointed to
the map and read off the coordinates of the area he wanted them to
move. When Ferrari was done writing them down in his notebook,
the company commander spoke again.

"Tell the drivers to go slow and use the hills to cover their
movement. I don't want a trail of dust kicked up. Once they get
there, set up some ambushes. If the Russians want Hauneck, they'll
have to pay for it. Pull 1st Platoon back here. I'll use them as a
reserve.

Oh - one more thing. From now on, let's use Blue for the bridge
and Orange for Hauneck. I can't pronounce these German names."

"Okay. That means we've only got two squads and O'Neal's
tanks up near Blue. Awful thin."

Sharp nodded. "Park the TOW vehicles along Route 4. I want
long range fire on anything coming towards us. Shoot and scoot.
That should help a bit."

Ferrari nodded as the plan took shape.

"Got it."

BAD OMENS

South of Bad Hersfeld, West Germany
0640

Sharp listened to the wall of echoes swept in from the east.

Hammer falls of artillery crashed over the land, causing the hills and valley to quake. Machine gun fire punctured the occasional gaps between the roar of tank guns. All around him was a ceaseless rumble, like driving fast through a tunnel with the windows rolled all the way down.

The constant din set off doubts in the back of his brain. Had he missed something? Soon enough, the battle would test his training and his plans. He only hoped he would be alive to apply the lessons in the next one.

Two glints of light crossed his vision. The signal from his two-man scout team indicated they were in place and had eyes to the east. From the top of the big hill, they could see whatever was coming towards them. To maintain radio silence, they were flashing the lights of their jeep using pre-arranged signals.

A pair of flagmen were positioned to the north and south along the valley, relaying Sharp's messages to the men at Blue and Orange respectively. Spreading out his men like this had complicated matters and made communication more difficult.

He wasn't even sure if he could send and receive clearly to Matheson, who was now busy digging in with his men in Hauneck. What a mess.

The loader's hatch creaked open, and Specialist Hartley's head popped up. His words sprawled out in a Texas twang.

"Sir, I'm getting something on two-oh-two."

Sharp slid a hand down and toggled the radio to the squadron net. The tinny buzz of foreign tongues sprang into his ear and then descended into static. Then a crashing series of heavy German syllables came over the radio only to be stepped on by a panicked mid-western voice.

"Pull back! All forces withdraw. We can't hold on here. There's just so many of them. We can't -."

A spray of static. Then silence.

Sharp set his tin of coffee on the turret deck and watched the dark ripples form in time with the distant splash of artillery. A tingle of fear ran down his spine as the cup clattered and toppled to the ground below. When he looked across the valley again, the jeep on the opposite hill flashed its lights in a wild series of blinks. Were the scouts sending a message or putting on a light show over there? Sure, they were excited, and that was understandable. But if Charlie Troop couldn't calm down and focus, they were all in big trouble. He swallowed a deep breath and counted to five before flicking the intercom switch and speaking to Private Hansen.

"Driver, I need you to flash your lights three times slow. Repeat. Three times. Slow."

Sharp watched and waited as the tank driver signaled to the scouts. After a short pause, the jeep flashed its lights in tight regular intervals.

F-R-I-E-N-D-L-I-E-S

"Got it…," he whispered. Over the intercom, he spoke to the tank's gunner. "Friendlies coming this way. Call out what you see. If something's not right, I want you to confirm it with me first."

Sergeant John Staudt's voice filled his headset. "Yes, sir."

Sharp ordered his driver to flash the headlights again. Through his binoculars, he watched the flagmen to the north and south relay his message to the platoon leaders. The message read simply:

H-O-L-D-F-I-R-E.

About a minute later, the first one came. The Abrams tank screamed backward along Route 4.

It looked really bad.

The front of the turret was battle-scarred with scorch marks. Along its track skirts, the olive-green paint had been stripped away revealing streaks of dull unfinished metal. It was as if a huge claw had raked the vehicle. Piled on the hull deck in a heap of human misery were wounded American and West German soldiers. Bloody unraveled bandages spilled off arms and legs. They huddled together in a clump of agony, so it was impossible to distinguish one man from another. The tank's loader sprayed a wild stream of rounds in the Abrams' wake. At last, the mangled vehicle rolled over the bridge near Blue and disappeared, wraith-like, to the west.

Next came a pair of M113 armored personnel carriers, one behind the other. The lead APC was dented as a battered Coke can. Just behind it was another M113. This one was missing its right track entirely. The bare road wheels just dug long steaming grooves into the asphalt surface. Sharp's gut clenched at the sickening sound, like nails against a chalkboard.

KREEEEEE!

The merciful end of this awful parade was marked by the appearance of an 8x8 German Luchs. Its autocannon was bent at a ninety-degree angle from the turret. Two of the wheels on the right side were gone. The vehicle veered across the wide autobahn lanes like a drunk coming out of a bar at three in the morning. Just short of the bridge near Objective Blue, the Luchs tilted on one side and capsized. A lone figure scrambled out of the turret hatch and staggered off the road before collapsing in the tall grass.

A sting of shame slapped Sharp as he watched the man lay there helpless. A fellow soldier was in trouble, and he could do nothing for him without revealing his position. He had to remind himself that if the roles were reversed, he would have wanted it that way.

His gaze returned to the scout position on the hill to the east. Long measured breaths kept the excitement and terror at bay. The jeep's lights flashed twice then twice again. This was it. The Russians were here.

Sharp changed frequency to the troop net and hit the "Push To Talk" button. The words flew out.

LIGHTNING SIX TO EYES ONE. GIVE ME A SITREP, OVER.

The radio crackled, and the scout on the opposite hill spoke in a breathless New York accent.

EYES ONE TO LIGHTNING SIX. SPOT REPORT. THIRTY T-80 TANKS MOVING WEST. REPEAT THREE ZERO TANGO EIGHT ZEROS. GRID 197292. OBSERVING. OVER.

The TOW vehicle element leader was the next one to speak up, confirming the sighting of the lead tanks rushing toward them down Autobahn Route 4. The grid reference placed the enemy at nearly three kilometers distance from their location. Three klicks. He had seen the TOW missiles fired in training before. They were deadly accurate. His thumb pressed down too hard on the "Push To Talk" button as his other hand balled into a tight fist.

LIGHTNING SIX TO LIGHTNING FOUR. MOVE UP TO INITIAL POSITIONS. CLEAR TO OPEN FIRE.

The TOW jeep and M901 sped down the highway, halted, and unleashed their ordnance. Thin tendrils of smoke snaked out from the missiles as they rushed ahead to find targets that Sharp couldn't see. Seconds later, two sick metallic slaps rang out along the valley. Sharp couldn't suppress a smile. Thick oily smoke near the reported enemy position drifted up into the blue sky. What came next was like honey to his ears.

LIGHTNING FOUR TO LIGHTNING SIX. CONFIRM TWO T-80 KILLS. SHOULD WE WITHDRAW NOW OR KEEP FIR-ING, OVER.

It was time to roll the dice. If they were facing thirty Russian tanks, he needed as many taken out as possible before they arrived here and overwhelmed his forces.

SIX TO FOUR. CLEAR TO FIRE AGAIN THEN PULL BACK TO BLUE, OVER.

A puff of smoke drifted over the overpass, marking the second volley of TOW missiles. Seconds later came the verbal confirmation T-80 kill. Sharp's blood was pumping. Thoughts and words spilled into his mind as the numbing fatigue slid off him. The TOW jeep and M901 seemed like sitting ducks out there on the overpass.

Although they were well out of range of the T-80 tank guns, they were wide open to artillery or air strike. The M901 was also unreliable with leaky hydraulics and unbalanced load. It was time to get them moving back. Over the squeals and static on the frequency, he shouted out his next order.

SIX TO FOUR. PULL BACK TO BLUE NOW, OVER.

Every sense was alive as the adrenaline of combat coursed through his veins. His men had just destroyed a platoon of Soviet tanks without suffering so much as a scratch. If the Russian commander was foolish enough to push down Route 4, he would find more of the same waiting for him. They would never reach that bridge. He and his men would leave their tanks strewn across the autobahn like hot garbage. Charlie Troop wasn't going to just win this battle. It was going to kick butt.

Over the hiss and pop of static, Sharp caught the scattered syllables of a spot report.

EYES ONE TO LIGHTNING SIX. SAY AGAIN. YOU'RE BREAKING UP.

No response.

Sharp glanced over at his three o'clock. Less than a dozen meters away, the four M1 tanks of 1st Platoon retreated from the tree line. Second Lieutenant Mike Wheal stood in his cupola directing his men through the glade behind them. Where the hell did they think they were going? He hadn't ordered any of them to reverse. Sharp flailed his arms and screamed in Wheal's direction.

"Hey! Did you get my last?"

The platoon leader ducked down in the tank, and the vehicle jolted to a halt.

"What?" shouted Wheal.

"Did you hear my last transmission?" Sharp shouted again. He pointed to his headset.

Wheal nodded. "Pull back to Blue, right?"

Sharp passed a palm over his face. Had he really just transmitted that order? He thought he had ordered only the TOW vehicles back to Blue. Either he had gotten too excited and miscommunicated, or the jamming had garbled his message enough to cause a misunderstanding. He shook his head.

"Stay here!" His own voice sounded cracked and broken.

Wheal waved at his tank commanders to halt their backward progress.

Worried that his other units may have misunderstood his previous order, Sharp ducked down into the tank and shut the hatch as a wave of static crashed through the frequency.

LIGHTNING SIX TO ALL UNITS. HALT. I SAY AGAIN HALT. ONLY LIGHTNING FOUR SHOULD WITHDRAW TO BLUE. REPEAT ONLY LIGHTNING FOUR. THOSE ARE THE TOW UNITS. EVERYONE ELSE STAY WHERE YOU ARE, OUT.

Bile rose up in Sharp's throat. Had that transmission been received? What was going on out there?

Things had started off so well but were falling apart quickly now. Why did he have to start messing around on the radio?

EYES ONE TO LIGHTNING SIX. SPOT REPORT -

His ears flooded with a sound like paper tearing at a thousand decibels. Sharp ripped off the combat helmet as a dagger of pain stabbed at his temple and then receded. "Damn you!" he shouted at the radio set. Some Russian signals flunky was out there playing with his electronic toys. Someday after the war ended, Sharp vowed to find him and turn him into a human pretzel.

Hartley looked at him with eyes as big as a half dollar. "You okay, sir?"

Sharp grunted as the blaring jet turbine in his head receded. Drips of rational thought fought their way back after a few long seconds. Jamming bad. Go back to the lights and flags? No. Too confusing. Change frequency. Hope.

He toggled the radio switch and spoke to the units once more.

LIGHTNING SIX TO ALL UNITS. SWITCH TO ALTERNATE FREQ. I WILL REPEAT ALL COMMANDS TWICE FROM NOW ON. IF YOU THINK I JUST GAVE YOU AN ORDER I WANT YOU TO CONFIRM IT WITH ME BEFORE YOU DO ANYTHING.

This was getting dangerous. Repeating his orders meant spending more time on the radio. That gave the enemy a better chance of finding him and dumping a hot load of artillery on his position.

"Hey, sir! I got something." It was Staudt, his gunner. "Movement up on that hill."

Sharp leaned forward to look through his primary sight extension, which showed precisely what Staudt was currently viewing. With the thermal mode turned on, the world was colored in a haze of deep green. The hill on the opposite side of the valley came into focus at ten times magnification. The dark outline of trees trembled. Hints of white-hot were visible among them. A second later, the source of the movement came into sight. Halfway down the slope, three T-80s were speeding down along a firebreak near Objective Orange. Sharp saw the danger immediately and radioed the scouts.

LIGHTNING SIX TO EYES ONE. ENEMY TANKS COMING STRAIGHT TOWARDS YOU. KEEP YOUR HEADS DOWN AND HOLD FIRE.

The lead T-80 didn't even slow when it came upon the scout jeep. Its right side hopped up and rolled right over the little vehicle. All that was left was a heap of junk.

Sharp bit his lip. That was our jeep. You are gonna pay for that.

"Staudt, line up a shot on the lead tank," he said. "What's your range?"

The gunner centered the black dot on the lead T-80. The laser rangefinder indicator blinked, and the digital readout underneath showed 2410 meters. Sharp slapped the top of Staudt's CVC and shouted over the whine of the tank's engine.

"Think you can hit it?"

"No problem!"

"Gunner! SABOT. Tank. Designate."

Staudt's reply shot out. "Identified."

Hartley banged a knee against his side panel. The steel door to his right slid open, and he pulled an armor-piercing round from the ready rack. With one smooth and practiced motion, he turned and hefted the sleek dark round into the breech.

"Up!" he shouted.

"Fire and adjust," shouted Sharp.

The turret rocked back as the tank's 105mm main gun hurled an armor piercing round that flew along at nearly sixteen football fields per second. Staudt announced the shot with a shrill yell.

"On the way!"

Sharp clenched his teeth. The thermal viewer showed the target's circular turret casing blow outward. A shower of thick bright sparks swept upward from the turret deck like a fountain. The T-80 stopped in the middle of the firebreak and sat there. Ten and twenty meters behind the wreck, the follow-on tanks halted.

"Hell yeah! He's gone," said Staudt.

Without enough room to advance down the narrow forest road, the only option for the tanks to get out of the kill zone was to reverse. Sharp saw the opportunity and grabbed it.

Using the manual turret override, the so-called "master blaster" joystick, he positioned the firing dot over the rear tank and ordered Staudt to take it out.

While the second shot was on the way, the turrets of both enemy tanks traversed, no doubt searching for whoever had shot up their platoon leader. They would never find out.

The M1's round carved into the hull deck of the rear tank. A bright emerald glow filled the thermal sight. When at last it dissipated, the T-80 was nothing but a heap of smoldering steel. The remaining enemy tank was caught between the two dead T-80s. It pivoted left and right, but the thick woods on either side blocked its progress. With nowhere to run, it just stopped moving and sat there.

In a bid to escape the fate of their comrades, the tank's surviving crewmen scrambled out from the hatches and leaped to the ground. Concealed in the nearby woods, the American scouts opened fire with their assault rifles. All three of the tank's crew members were cut down. Staudt lined up the shot carefully and fired a third time. The T-80 turret flung ten feet in the air as a column of flame leaped from the metal corpse. Sharp couldn't help but think the crewmen had been lucky to die from the rifles instead of getting caught in the inferno.

As he leaned back from the sight, he suddenly realized someone had been repeating his callsign over the radio net. A pair of voices flooded into Sharp's headset, neither intelligible. It sounded a lot like Second Lieutenant O'Neal and First Lieutenant Ferrari were stepping over each other's transmissions.

That meant something was up at Blue. It was time to stop playing tank commander and get back to leading his company. A quick radio message to Wheal in 1st Platoon unleashed his tanks to open fire on any other enemies that were so foolish as to try and come over the distant hill.

Ferrari spoke up again. This time O'Neil stayed quiet and let the XO speak.

LIGHTNING SIX ONE TO LIGHTNING SIX. WE CAN HEAR FIRING TO THE SOUTH. IS THAT FROM YOU, OVER.

Sharp cursed at Schnauffer for giving such a broad area of operations. One half of the troop couldn't even tell what the other half was busy doing.

SIX TO SIX ONE. THAT'S US FIRING. WE HAD ENEMY CONTACT AT KILO SEVEN. GIVE ME A SITREP. ANY ENEMY CONTACT?

The reply rang of deep disappointment.

NEGATIVE.

Sharp's attention was yanked away when one of Wheal's tanks bellowed, followed by a second and a third shot. With his heart thumping, he popped up in the cupola to see what was going on. Down in the valley, two T-80s with mine plows sat burning to the east of Hauneck. In their wake lay a rough path carved out of the forested hillside. A dozen tanks poured through the breach in the thick vegetation. The Soviet commander, unable to find a suitable road that led down the hill, had evidently decided to create his own. Sharp's gut filled with the horror of his awful miscalculation. They were not coming straight down the road for Blue. Instead, the Russians were coming over the hills toward Orange.

A grassy patch of ground in front of Wheal's tank erupted. Clods of dirt and grass whipped up into the air. The enemy tanks were shooting back. The nerve of them!

An enemy round clanged off the turret of Wheal's Abrams, leaving a dark scorch mark where it had hit. The turret hydraulics whined as the main gun swiveled right then left and then stopped moving. The commander's hatch flipped up, and a tuft of smoke billowed upwards from the guts of the tank. First Lieutenant Wheal, coughing and wheezing, climbed out and slid off the turret.

The loader and driver were next to evacuate. Sharp held his breath and waited for the gunner. Nothing. It was time to call an ambulance.

LIGHTNING SIX TO LIGHTNING SIX TWO. TAKING CASUALTIES. REQUEST MEDEVAC IMMEDIATELY. GRID 190212.

Wheal staggered over to Sharp's Abrams and leaned heavily on the hull deck.

"You hurt?" said Sharp.

Wheal shook his head after another spasm of coughing wracked his ribs.

Sharp gestured to the lieutenant's tank. "Your gunner okay?"

Wheal looked over at the crippled beast and counted his men. The loader crouched on the ground, nursing his left elbow while the driver gulped from a canteen. The lieutenant's eyes went wide, and he ran back to his men and slapped them on the shoulder. The three of them climbed up on the Abrams together. Wheal dove in through the hatch, followed by the driver. Seconds later, both men emerged, each with his hand hooked under the gunner's armpits. The kid screamed and cried through a smoke-scarred face, and his charred limbs shook with agony the whole time.

As Wheal and the driver lay the man down on a bed of tall grass, Sharp scanned the western side of the hill, hoping to catch a glimpse of the armored ambulance. Of course, it had to come all the way from Objective Blue - something he hadn't considered earlier in the planning stages. The bad decisions seemed to be mounting, and he sensed the entire battle getting ahead of him. Like a sleepwalker on a ledge, he would need to wake up before he fell to his fate.

Initiative.

He needed to stop reacting and do something right now. Something no one would expect.

Sharp keyed the radio and spoke to First Sergeant Ray Matheson, who was probably sitting at Objective Orange with his two squads and watching a flood of enemy tanks coming his way.

LIGHTNING SIX TO LIGHTNING BLUE ONE. I'M SENDING FRIENDLY ARMOR YOUR WAY. WATCH YOUR FIRE AND HOLD ON. WE'RE COMING.

POOR BLOODY INFANTRY

Objective Orange

Branching off Route 4 was Highway 27, which shot south then curved west, eventually leading to Route 7. A ten minute's leisurely drive north would then lead to an overpass that hooked west again onto Route 5. At the end of that road was the biggest prize in Western Europe - the city of Frankfurt, where sat the headquarters of US V Corps and the central nervous system of American military units in West Germany. Once the city fell, the war would be pretty much over, and NATO would be forced to call it quits, launch the nukes, or fall back into France.

Of course, knowing all this didn't help First Sergeant Ray Matheson one bit. Almost an hour ago, Captain Sharp had given him two squads of infantry and tasked them with the job of stopping a flood of Russian tanks from charging south through here. The troop commander, in his infinite wisdom, had told him to set up shop in the north of Eitra, which had a commanding view of Route 27 all the way up to Route 4. From here, they were to fire off a few long-range Dragon missiles at the flanks of any T-80s that would inevitably thunder straight down Route 4 towards Bad Hersfeld. After taking out a few tanks, Matheson would call it a day and return to Objective Blue when it was time to blow the bridge.

It was just too bad that the Russians hadn't been notified of Captain Sharp's game plan. Instead, they had insisted on charging over the large wooded hill to the east of Eitra. From the window sill on the second floor of an abandoned stone house, he counted nearly a dozen tanks scuttling along the valley floor toward his position. They were no more than a kilometer away, but he had no trouble making out the low hull with the flat circular turrets dotted with explosive armor. With a half-dozen LAW rockets and two Dragon missile launchers, the idea of holding his position here seemed like a sick joke.

Sharp's briefing had been muddy about his intent and the answers Matheson got to his questions went around in circles. That wasn't like Sharp at all. The sergeant suspected the problems were rooted somewhere higher up the chain and he was willing to bet that Schnauffer had made too many promises again. It was time to reach out and touch someone. The only problem was that the radio didn't work at all here and when it did, Sharp was busy moving guys back and forth like chess pieces. The church tower to the south offered some promise. Perhaps if he could get there and talk to the troop commander and explain the situation, the guy would come to his senses and send some armor his way or order the infantry to pull back. Anything was better than sitting here and getting shot to pieces.

"Jasper," he muttered. "Get over here."

From behind him, a thick nasal buzz drifted across the faint chill breeze.

"Dammit, Jasper!" shouted Matheson.

The kid's eyes shot open, and he jumped up. A line of drool ran from his lower lip all the way down to his combat webbing.

"Private Jasper," said the sergeant. "Last time I caught you sleeping on the job, what was your punishment?"

The kid stood frozen, his eyes wandering along the contours of the room as if the answer were scrawled on the bedroom's eggshell white walls.

"Uh...sergeant, you ordered me to vacuum the barracks parking lot."

"And when the cord didn't reach all the way to an outlet, what did I make you do next?"

Jasper mumbled. "Sergeant Matheson, you ordered me to make vacuuming noises."

"That's damn right. And if you think I'm not gonna make you do it again just cause we're in a battle, then you are mistaken. You'll be out there dodging Russian tank rounds with a vacuum in your hands."

Three long strides later, Jasper was beside Matheson. The tremble of the private's lower lip told the sergeant all he needed to know. The men still feared him more than they did the Russians. Excellent.

He brought the handset of the PRC-77 portable radio to his ear and listened in on the alternate frequency. What he heard was a low static buzz that resembled a band saw. They would have to try again from the church tower.

"Private Jasper, you see that building down the block? We're gonna take this hunka junk radio over there and get up in the tower. I need to make a call over to Captain Sharp and report our situation and ask for reinforcements."

The kid said nothing. He just tightened the straps of the portable radio on his back.

Matheson swiveled toward the other members of 3rd Platoon's A and B squads. Camo-streaked faces stared back at him. Matheson had endured two tours of duty in the Central Highlands of Vietnam and was no stranger to combat. He knew what they were going through right now. Each of them was dealing with the fear of failing their friends. Despite all their training, the men carried shreds of self-doubt as to whether they would actually perform in the moment of truth. As the wayward grandpa of Charlie Troop, there was little the sergeant could say or do now to help these guys. The enemy was on the way. The only thing left to do was to ride the chaos.

"Listen up. I want the two Dragon teams up on the rooftops. Here and across the road. Hit the tanks coming towards us. Don't worry about which ones. There's plenty to choose from. Don't stay in one place! Fire off a round then move quick as you can down the block. Fall back and do it again from the dug-in positions.

The rest of you set up shop in the houses and use your LAWs when the tanks come this way. Remember - rear shots only. Those '80s are way too thick on the sides and front. Sergeant Tomlinson's in charge 'til I get back."

Words would do no more good here. Matheson grabbed the M16 rifle, and a LAW then ran down the stairs as the men went to work.

Jasper and Matheson jogged down the sleepy suburban street. The quaint homes of Eitra, lined up in neat little rows along the east side of the highway, shook with the roar of a tank's main gun booming somewhere off to the northwest. Matheson shot a look back to make sure Jasper was keeping up. The kid's lanky frame clopped along as if he were warming up for the track team.

"Let's go, private!" shouted Matheson.

Both men hopped a white picket fence and ran south along the single road that led up the hill towards the centuries-old church just to the southeast of the town. Its tower sat there like a beacon of hope. With any luck, Matheson would be able to get hold of Sharp and count off the targets for him to hit. If they were fortunate, Sharp would pull them out of here and blow the bridges - to hell with Schnauffer's half-baked orders.

Halfway down the main thoroughfare, the growl of a tank's diesel engine caught Matheson's ears. He sprinted for cover behind the corner of a small bank. Smiling family faces in the window assured him that there had never been a better time to take out a mortgage.

WHAM!

The facade of the restaurant down the block crumpled and slid to the ground. Matheson's ears rang from the blast of the nearby tank gun. It was time to get away from the street. He snagged the private's collar and yanked him along the alley. A few steps later, they were in a little parking lot behind the bank surrounded by the blank exterior walls of single-story shops.

Matheson shook his head. You had to hand it to the Europeans. They were the only people in the world who could build a town right here in a spacious valley and then cram the buildings this close together. A dark metal door marked the rear employee entrance to one of the buildings. Matheson hammered at it with the butt of his M16 to no avail.

Jasper spoke up. "What do we do, Sergeant Matheson?"

Their options were limited, to say the least. If they went back out in the street, the T-80 would probably turn them both into a fine paste. If they stayed here like this, the whole town would be full of tanks pretty soon and moving along the roads would be impossible. Matheson glanced around at the low buildings and shrugged.

"Okay, I got an idea. Let's get up on the roof. We'll move along the tops of the buildings."

Jasper's face lit up. "Like ninjas!"

"Sure. Whatever."

Jasper boosted the squat sergeant up on his six-foot seven frame, allowing Matheson a handhold on the mottled brick ledge of a flower shop. A few grunts and curses later, he was up. Matheson extended a hand down, and the skinny private from Kansas found his footing after falling down only twice. From up here, Matheson sighted the tank sitting in the middle of the narrow street. Over to the west were A and B squad's positions.

The Dragon missile's launch was announced by a drumbeat of air. Off near the hills to the east, a T-80 mine plow disappeared in a fireball. A second later came the explosion followed by a shock wave. The T-80 on the street rotated its turret towards the Dragon crew's position. Matheson covered his ears as the gun blared, but it did little to stop the ringing that followed. The roof of the house blew outwards in a stony hail of fragments.

"Holy crow," shouted Jasper.

Matheson swore as the building disintegrated in chunks. Somewhere among the rubble were his men. The sergeant's mind was made up. The T-80 needed to die.

"You got your LAW?"

Jasper nodded and turned around to show him. The short cylinder was tucked beneath the radio's manpack.

"Okay, son. Let's go."

Both men ran in a crouch along the rooftops until they were nearly even with the T-80's position on the street. From up here, Matheson had a clear shot at the tank almost directly below. The two antennae at the rear marked it as a possible command tank.

He chuckled, knowing that he was about to vaporize an officer. It had been that kind of day for Sergeant Matheson.

"When I get to three, I want you to fire," he told Jasper. "Aim for the turret hatch."

Matheson counted off. Just before he reached three, the rocket wooshed out of Jasper's launcher tube and slammed into the top of the turret. A chunk of explosive reactive armor detonated. Shards of metal slapped the building. A searing pain bit into Matheson's hand. Embedded in the back of it was a jagged piece of smoking metal. He chomped down hard on his tongue and pressed the trigger bar on the LAW's launcher tube.

The second rocket smacked down hard on the tank, right where Jasper's had hit only seconds before. This time, without a plate of reactive armor, the projectile burrowed deep into the turret and ignited like fireworks. The stench of burnt electronics seeped up through the hole, carried along by belches of ink-black smoke. For the first time in a long while, Matheson felt the edges of his lips move upward.

With his face turned away from Jasper, he shouted. "Come on, dough head! Let's get to the church!"

"But sarge - your hand!"

Matheson pointed to the burning tank below. "Don't make me send you down there to clean up that mess!"

Both men stood up and ran along the roof. The agony seeped in as the adrenaline wore off with each passing second. By the time they neared the church, the sergeant's tongue bled from biting down on it so hard. To his surprise, the huge double doors of the holy place creaked open with the simple turn of a knob.

It was dark inside. Matheson raised his M16, half-expecting to be cut down by a hail of enemy rounds. Instead, a wave of anguished cries swept toward him. A child's shriek. A woman's gasp.

When his eyes finally adjusted to the light, his gut clenched and his rifle lowered as he realized what he was looking at. Nearly a dozen civilians sat in the pews. Who were these people? Why on Earth were they still here?

Down the aisle strode a young priest adorned in vestments. His English came out haltingly but was passable - at least much better than Matheson's German.

"We cannot get out…Help us?"

Matheson let out a long breath. What was he going to do with these civvies? He couldn't just leave them behind in the middle of a warzone. If the artillery came in, this whole town would cease to exist. Or at the very least they would be trapped here when the bridges to the west were blown. Then they'd be left to fend for themselves in enemy-occupied territory. It would be just like leaving South Vietnam again. After that conflict, he had told himself the same two words that so many others who had fought there had said to themselves. "Never again."

Matheson didn't even need a second to think about it. The response was knee-jerk.

"We'll get you out of here," he told the priest. "Don't worry about that."

He gestured upward to the church tower then pointed to the radio on Private Jasper's back. After a few seconds, it became apparent what Matheson wanted. The German priest led them behind the altar and unlocked a heavy wooden door concealed just behind a statue of Saint Michael.

Both Americans climbed up the steep and narrow staircase. Matheson's hand pulsed and he considered yanking out the fragment, but he already knew that would spell more trouble. Soon enough, he'd have someone take a look at it. Or he'd be dead. So there was really no more point in thinking about it, was there? He mentally squeezed the door shut on the shooting pains as they radiated up through his arm and set fire to his brain.

The top of the bell tower offered a breath-taking view of the battle that stretched over the valley and into the hills to the west. Wheal's 1st Platoon lit up with muzzle flashes as the Abrams tanks poured fire into the onrushing T-80s below. Despite all the hulks of Soviet vehicles that were littered and strewn all over the valley, the remainder rushed westward without stopping.

Matheson yanked the radio handset from Jasper's hands and spoke up.

LIGHTNING BLUE ONE TO LIGHTNING SIX. T-80S COMING WEST FROM OUR CURRENT POSITION NEAR OBJECTIVE ORANGE. WE ARE OVERRUN HERE. ALSO HAVE CIVILIANS WHO REQUIRE EVAC IMMEDIATELY, OVER.

No response.

Matheson angled the whip-like antenna towards the west and repeated himself. Through the wall of static, Sharp's accented voice responded.

LIGHTNING SIX TO LIGHTNING BLUE ONE. I'M SENDING FRIENDLY ARMOR YOUR WAY. WATCH YOUR FIRE AND HOLD ON. WE'RE COMING.

FLANK HITS

Objective Blue

The bridge near Eichhofsiedlung was loaded with no less than thirty kilograms of shaped charges on its central supports. Dozens of explosive packs were set under the cross girders on the east and west sides. One of the combat engineers had dug into a big rucksack and produced four plastic bags filled with something that looked a lot like orange gelatin. The other sappers gleefully planted these under the columns on either end. Before boarding the Huey helicopter with the rest of his team, they had assured Lieutenant Ferrari that when the bridge blew, it was going to be "totally awesome."

Of that, he had no doubt.

But for now, the bridge sat there, serene as a late summer day. Everything in the little suburb of Bad Hersfeld was quiet. The flat valley floor to the east was unmarred by the sight of enemy tanks. Behind him, the men of O'Neal's Abrams platoon sat with their tanks behind high berms. The two TOW vehicles sat nearby while their crews recounted taking out the lead Soviet tank platoon.

It was enough to drive Ferrari nuts.

Where were the Russian tanks he was promised? When would his war start? This was, after all, what he had spent his whole adult life training to do.

The guest lectures at West Point had invited speakers to come and speculate at length about World War III. Although none of the senior officers could agree on the specifics of how the war would be fought, they all agreed on one thing - that it would be decided in a matter of days rather than months or years.

A sick falling sensation settled in his gut.

What if the war ended and he hadn't fired a shot? After this was over and the Americans won, the path to promotion would be set. The doors to the upper echelons of the officer corps would swing open only to those who had seen combat. After-action reports would dictate who shot up towards the pinnacle of the army and those left behind. Since entering The Point as a bean head six years ago, Ferrari had stars in eyes - four of them, to be exact. He had always seen himself on a straight-line trajectory towards a Pentagon posting and the pride it would bring his parents. Now those stars were falling and his future seemed dim.

A series of powerful blasts rang out. First Lieutenant Ralph Ferrari was eight years old on Christmas morning all over again.

Clutching the radio in a death grip of excited optimism, he spoke to Captain Sharp, the company commander.

LIGHTNING SIX ONE TO LIGHTNING SIX. WE CAN HEAR FIRING TO THE SOUTH. IS THAT FROM YOU, OVER.

The radio crackled and bleated like a truck horn. Another volley of tank fire rolled like thunder to the south. Sharp's voice sizzled in a faint hazy fog of interference.

SIX TO SIX ONE. THAT'S US FIRING. WE HAD ENEMY CONTACT AT KILO SEVEN. GIVE ME A SITREP. ANY ENEMY CONTACT ALONG ROUTE 4?

Ferrari tossed the binoculars in front of him and sighed. How was he going to spin the combat report? The single sentence referencing to his contribution to the fight took shape in his head. "XO Ferrari maintained secure defensive line at Objective Blue." Who wouldn't see through that? This was awful. He pushed the transmit button and let the lonely single-word fall out of his mouth.

NEGATIVE.

Thirty seconds later, Sharp requested a medevac near his position and Ferrari waved the APC forwards. Ferrari's fingers drummed on the deck as he watched it disappear over the hill. If 1st Platoon was taking losses then maybe soon the troop commander would need reinforcements. He knew it was a horrible thought, but he couldn't fight it any longer. Route 4 was empty of targets. He needed new ones.

The troop net came alive with Sergeant Matheson's gravel voice. He sounded angry and annoyed, which was pretty much par for the course for the company sergeant.

LIGHTNING BLUE ONE TO LIGHTNING SIX. T-80S COMING WEST FROM OUR CURRENT POSITION NEAR OBJECTIVE ORANGE. WE ARE OVERRUN HERE. ALSO HAVE CIVILIANS WHO REQUIRE EVAC IMMEDIATELY, OVER.

Did he hear that right? Civilians? T-80s? And here he was, sitting pretty in an APC with nothing to do. Well, if he was going to get anything done in this war, he was going to have to take the initiative. Ferrari tried to frame a request in his head as Sharp replied to Matheson.

LIGHTNING SIX TO LIGHTNING BLUE ONE. I'M SENDING FRIENDLY ARMOR YOUR WAY. WATCH YOUR FIRE AND HOLD ON. WE'RE COMING.

A flurry of orders came back and forth. O'Neal's tanks rumbled east down Route 4 to provide a flanking attack against the oncoming T-80s. Objective Blue was stripped bare of its heavy punch with only two squads of infantry and a couple of TOW vehicles that were both low on ammo. He smiled in hopeful anticipation as he spoke up.

LIGHTNING SIX TWO TO LIGHTNING SIX. DO YOU NEED ANY TRANSPORT FOR THOSE CIVILIANS? I'LL GO OVER THERE AND HELP OUT, OVER.

A long minute of silence was broken by a mere handful of words that set him free.

GO AHEAD, SIX ONE. MOVE FAST.

Ferrari didn't need to be told twice. He shouted at the driver, who slammed on the accelerator. The sudden jolt nearly gave the XO a whiplash as the APC jerked forward and stumbled off the pavement of Route 4.

Ahead of him, O'Neal's four Abrams tanks rumbled along in echelon right formation. As they cleared the base of the long hill, his thoughts froze at the sight that lay before him. The entire valley was more or less on fire with vehicles that lay in crumpled heaps of jagged burning metal. On the long hill to the south, Sharp and three tanks from 1st Platoon were slowly reversing west, firing again and again at the rushing mass of Soviet steel. The front hull of one of the nearest T-80s flashed as a 105mm round struck home. The Russian tank shook a little then stopped. It did not move again.

The three Abrams on the hill pulled back again as another volley of enemy tank fire hurtled at them. Three of the T-80 platoons moved forward in neat formations while the others stopped and fired. The timing of the fire and movement looked well-practiced. Like a lion charging towards its prey, the Russians rushed straight towards 1st Platoon's tanks, which were reversing up the hill as they fired. Caught between the Soviets to the east and the river to the west, they would soon run out of room to maneuver. Clearly, the Soviet battalion commander had seen it too. The only problem was that his platoons were in line abreast formation with no flanking cover. A fatal mistake.

O'Neal's platoon wheeled around the right flank of the Russians, unleashing armor-piercing rounds while on the move. A pair of T-80s nearly half a kilometer away erupted in flames. One of the enemy vehicles exploded a second time - then a third - as the ammunition inside the turret cooked off. Though Ferrari was being thrown around in the cupola of his M113, he still had the capacity to whoop and holler.

The confusion among the enemy set in almost immediately. The T-80s halted as if some great hand had yanked back on their leash. The tight formations sprawled outward. Several of the T-80s reversed while others remained motionless. Sharp's tanks took advantage of the chaos and engaged the nearest three-tank platoon. One of the rounds punched a fist-sized hole in the front hull of the lead tank. The top hatch flipped open, and the tank commander climbed up, only to crumple when a stream of coaxial machine gun fire drummed into him. Armored vehicles started exploding all along the valley floor as O'Neal's tanks joined in again.

The enemy tanks fired back, but the shots were wild, crashing into the hillside or landing to the north near Bad Hersfeld.

Ferrari ordered his driver to swing south along Route 27. The APC weaved around the remains of a T-80's turret. The end of the main gun was stuck in the soft ground like a thrown spear. Something cut through the air just above his head and a split second later, the hill to his left bellowed with the impact of an incoming tank round. A geyser of dirt heaved upward. Ferrari hunched in the cupola as the fragments of earth splashed down on his helmet. The APC kept right on going through the dark shower. By the time it emerged from the dirty cloud, the deck of the M113 was as black as coal.

"Dear god, I could start a garden up here!" he shouted. As the tracked vehicle reached halfway to Hauneck, the radio crackled to life.

DARKHORSE TO ALL UNITS. WITHDRAW WEST OF THE RIVER. SAY AGAIN, PULL BACK ACROSS THE RIVER. EXECUTE ALPHA ONE, OVER.

Ferrari shrugged. The order had come straight from Schnauffer. It was crystal clear. It was time to get the heck out of Dodge. Civilians or not, pressing on towards Orange would be violating orders. What would THAT look like in the report? It was time to get his tin can turned around. He flipped the radio switch and spoke to Sharp, informing that he was complying with the major's order.

LIGHTNING SIX ONE TO LIGHTNING SIX. WITHDRAWING AS ORDERED, OVER.

The APC slowed down and turned off the pavement just a few dozen meters short of a smoking T-80. Its tracks were sheared off and lay uncoiled on the ground like a garden snake. Ferrari's attention was wrenched away by a grizzly bark.

LIEUTENANT FERRARI IF YOU DON'T GET YOUR BUTT OVER HERE RIGHT NOW, I WILL PERSONALLY FIND YOU WHEN THIS IS ALL OVER AND I WILL DO SOME DAMAGE. DO YOU HEAR ME, YOU LITTLE WEST POINT PUKE?!

Ferrari's imagination ran wild with the probabilities. Sergeant Matheson was a decorated Vietnam veteran who had been killing communists since the XO was in diapers.

Between the scores of Soviet tanks that swarmed all around him and Matheson, he knew whom he feared more.

"Turn back!" he screamed to the driver.

The APC circled again and swept south through the thick dark fog. The metallic clangs of battle rang in his ears, but Ferrari couldn't even make out the source of the clatter. The M113 sped down the roads of Eitra. On Ferrari's left, just past the burning troop carriers of 3rd Platoon lay neat little rows of houses that lined the long street that led to the town church. The hulk of a T-80 tank sat in the middle of a nearby road. A gaping hole had been punched in its turret.

The M113 pulled up to the church. The executive officer climbed out as the rear ramp clattered to the street. Ten sheepish steps later, he knocked twice on the double doors of the holy place and waited. When the doors swung open, he was greeted by the weary and weathered face of First Sergeant Matheson. He was covered head-to-toe in ash. A half-smoked cigarette stuck out of his mouth, and a jagged piece of metal dug into the back of his hand.

A crowd of civilians stood behind him.

Matheson reached over and thrust a screaming baby at Lieutenant Ferrari.

"Good morning, sir," said the First Sergeant. "Nice of you to stop by for a visit."

BURNING BRIDGES

The sickly smell of burning tanks permeated the whole valley. Sharp lit a Marlboro, but even that couldn't mask the stench. Despite that, there were other benefits. With each puff, his hands shook just a little less and his thoughts cleared. They had made it - but only just barely. The last of the Soviet T-80s had been destroyed two minutes ago. Any time now, the second echelon would appear, and they would have to do it all over again if they were not out of here soon. That was out of the question.

His Abrams couldn't face another such battle right now. The dials in front of him were all leaning hard to the left. The rate of fire had peaked five minutes ago then slackened as everyone realized that the ready racks were as empty as a pew on Friday night. After frantically loading round after round into the breech, Specialist Hartley was now nursing his shoulder. The guy just didn't have enough gas left in the tank to lift and swing the big heavy rounds.

Charlie Troop was also near its breaking point. Radio calls were taking too long for a reply and what was coming back were exhausted and slurred responses. Communication was breaking down, and Sharp wasn't even sure where his XO had gone or if he was still alive. The last he heard, Ferrari had asked permission to go pick up Matheson and his men near Objective Blue. After that, the troop sergeant was shouting at the XO over the radio. If it came up again, Sharp would say that he hadn't heard the exchange.

He couldn't afford to lose Matheson.

Although Sharp hated to admit it, Schnauffer was right. It was time to get out of here. The only problem was that almost nobody was anywhere near they were supposed to be.

O'Neal's tanks, which should have been back at Objective Blue, were now tearing straight south down Route 27, finishing off any surviving Russian tanks with a second helping of armor-piercing. Ferrari and Matheson were pulling civilians and two infantry squads out of Hauneck. The only people who were in position were the handful of troops and the TOW vehicles he'd left in Eichofsiedlung. He needed his people to drop whatever they were doing and consolidate across the river. It had to happen five minutes ago.

LIGHTNING SIX TO ALL ELEMENTS. WITHDRAW TO OBJECTIVE BLUE. I SAY AGAIN, STOP WHATEVER YOU ARE DOING AND GET BACK TO BLUE. THAT IS A DIRECT ORDER, OVER.

Sharp sighed and shook his head. The interference and jamming hadn't slackened one bit since the start of the battle. He couldn't be sure if anybody had actually received his order or if he was missing their responses. Even with the yellow smoke swirling around his tank, he couldn't know if anyone saw the signal to pull back. Schnuaffer's voice shot over the radio once again.

DARKHORSE TO LIGHTNING SIX. ARE YOU SECURE? WE NEED TO MOVE NOW.

Far to the north, a plume of blue smoke drifted upwards from Schnauffer's position. With both visual and verbal commands coming in, it was getting harder by the minute to delay. Sharp told his driver to move north and cross the bridge. As the tanks of 1st Platoon drove on ahead, he turned in the cupola to take one last look at the hell on Earth he had created.

The carcasses of bludgeoned steel were strewn all the way from Hauneck to the base of the hill where he and Mike Wheal's men had made their stand. Only a bare hundred meters away sat two platoons of burning T-80s. The obscene funeral pyre marked the point at which the wave of angry men and steel had finally broken. Wheal's tank sat there in front of them as if it were mocking the enemy.

He hoped the whole scene stayed there like that for the rest of the entire damn war. Mess with the Cav, this is what you get.

The valley to the east came alive with the deep grumble of tank engines. Not just a company either. A stampede was headed his way, and there just didn't seem to be enough time for his men to fall back. He crossed over the bridge, relieved to find at least a few of his men still here and waiting in their defensive positions. Over the muddy banks of the Fulda River, the bridge sat there ready to go at a word's notice. A whip-like crack from the north and south signaled the destruction of the other key bridges. Only Blue was left standing. Schnauffer would have questions and Sharp needed to formulate answers quick.

Ferrari's box-like command APC hooked west on to Route 4. O'Neal's tanks and another APC were not far behind. A pair of tank rounds slapped into the facade of a McDonald's, sending the facade - golden arches and all - tumbling to the Earth. A pair of Abrams swung their turrets south and loosened their rounds in the direction of whatever had just fired at them.

Sharp grabbed his binoculars for a better look at Ferrari's command APC. On top of it were the remnants of A and B squad. Men clung to the deck in a heap. Legs and arms dangled off the side of the vehicle as it pressed west toward the bridge. The only explanation for their presence on top of the vehicle would be that civilians were riding inside.

The men behind Sharp shouted encouragement as the vehicles chugged steadily down the autobahn. Cries of "Come on!" and "Let's go!" rang out all along Objective Blue. Finally, the APCs and the tanks crossed the bridge just as Schnauffer's shouts reached a crescendo of rage.

The engineers had left behind a detonator for Sharp. It was brown and plastic with a single red button, which made it look a lot like a toy. Sharp wondered if it was even going to work as he extended the telescoping metal antenna at the top and urged the men to get back. The columns under the bridge heaved, and the cross girders disintegrated with the first blast. The eastern section of the bridge plummeted into the river while the west side hesitated for a moment then decided to topple to the right.

When the smoke cleared, the entire thing was just another memory.

Sharp turned to see the medics leaning over Mike Wheal's gunner. One of them looked up at the company commander and shook his head. He wanted to say something about this kid from some small town, but there was just no time. Charlie Troop left the bridge behind and passed west, leaving a trail of death and destruction behind them. The sting of a near failure bit deep. He had miscalculated the enemy, and one of his men had paid the price for it. Next time, he promised himself, he would do better.

Next time.

RAZVEDKA

Mengshausen Kuppe, West Germany
473 meters above sea level

Vasily and his men had stumbled upon it by pure chance.

Ivan had been driving the BRDM back and forth along the old mining roads that slithered along the hillsides to the east of the objective. When the team stopped to get its bearings, Petro's sharp eye caught sight of the flat circular roof that sat above the treetops. A few minutes of walking and they were at its base. Suddenly the mood shifted from sullen to celebratory.

Together they bounded up the spiraling staircase of the observation tower hidden among the thickly forested hills.

When he reached the highest platform, Vasily laughed like a child with a new toy.

From here, his four-man reconnaissance "razvedka" team had a breathtaking view of the landscape to the west. It couldn't have been more perfect.

That the Americans had not managed to secure this vital piece of real estate was perplexing. Perhaps they had forgotten about it. Their loss would be his gain.

Vasily grabbed the binoculars that hung around his neck and gazed west. He could see down into the valley and over the quiet little German town of Mengshausen. Beyond it lay the bridge that spanned the Fulda River. Nestled against the western bank were the little houses of Niederaula, a farming community that had sat there undisturbed for centuries. It was obvious why the place needed to be captured. Not only was there a precious river crossing here but it was also a junction where three major roads converged. Seizing them would ease the growing military traffic jam that built up behind them by the minute.

Petro stepped up to the top floor and stretched.

"What a sight!" he shouted. He sat down on the cold metal floor and removed his priceless camera equipment and sketchbooks from the bag.

Vasily gave him a big grin and tossed him a pack of cigarettes. It was a small reward for finding this place.

"Ivan's waiting down in the car?" he asked.

Petro nodded. "Alen's coming soon. Can you see the objective from here?"

"Yes. I can see everything from up here. Don't smoke those now. Someone will see the flame."

Alen clambered up next. A long line of telephone cable unspooled behind him. The usual sneer sliced across his face.

"I don't see what the big deal is," he said. "It's just a single small bridge and a few roads."

Vasily couldn't bear it. Did he need to spell out everything to this mudak?

"Try to imagine what's happening behind us," he said. "Every minute we don't advance is another minute where a tank company pulls up to a long line of vehicles and sits idle. It's as if your babushka kept feeding you potato stew for days and wouldn't let you go to the bathroom even once. Soon, you would be very sick from such constipation."

Alen gestured out toward Nieduraula and shrugged. "So what am I looking at here then?"

Vasily pointed out the three major roads that converged in the city and branched out west. "What you are looking at," he said, "is the enema."

Without further argument, the team went about its work.

Vasily tucked in the forest-green blanket and admired the results. If anyone bothered to look up here, they would see only a dirty pile of branches and grass that had swept in from the nearby trees. It wasn't perfect, but Vasily had learned in Afghanistan that a casual observer could be fooled by even minimal concealment. Put another way, human beings saw what they wanted to see.

Petro lay prone under the thick wool and peered through the viewfinder of his Kiev 88. Like the rest of the team's equipment, the antique camera was blessed with a kind of rugged simplicity. Just twenty minutes ago, he had used its zoom function to find a hidden path sliced into the hills east of Hauneck. Now he was using it to sniff out the American ambush positions nearby. Before Vasily could put the finishing touches on the hide, the little Ukranian had spotted something.

"American command tank," Petro announced. "Flashing its headlights to communicate. They make it so easy!"

Petro read off the grid reference to Alen, who scribbled them down in his pad and spoke the numbers into the bulky field telephone. Down at the base of the tower, Ivan sat in the BRDM-2 listening and repeating the numbers into the vehicle's powerful radio set. That information would be collected by someone at battalion level and compared with the data from the three other Soviet recon teams that were spread out around here. Once the picture was complete, it would be churned through a series of mind-bending mathematical formulas and used to plan the coming operation.

It all came down to numbers and formulas and charts. Conducting modern conventional war in any other way was suicide.

Vasily taped over the lenses of his binoculars until only a slit was left. This would hamper his view, but it was a necessary measure to prevent a glint of sunlight from reflecting off the glass. Once he was satisfied that the lenses wouldn't betray his position, he peered down into the valley through the fields. Sure enough, the soft soil to the northeast was marked by the impression of a tread. No doubt the Americans were dug in somewhere near the tall pine trees, but it was hard to say what kind of vehicles were there.

Vasily nudged Petro. "The fields on the left. Near the gas station. Tread marks. See them?"

"Yes. What about it?"

"Come on, you know what I mean. What made that mark?"

Petro let the suspense go on for seconds longer than he needed. Vasily had discovered the young man's penchant for drama when they first worked together in the snow-capped mountains of Paktia Province. Every time Vasily had asked him to do something, Petro made it seem like it was a heavy burden on his talent. He would hum and haw about this or that question when he had already clearly known the answer.

Vasily let him play his little game without complaint. After all, Petro was the only other man in the team that was still alive from those days. Alen and Ivan were recent additions, and neither of them had seen war up close until this morning. Technically, Alen outranked all of them, but no one wanted to listen to him.

After all, he was a sheep herder from Kazahk! He barely spoke Russian well enough to borrow a lighter - never mind command a team.

"Too light for an Abrams," said Petro. "15-inch track width. M113. Wait. No. See those little rectangular prints near where the tracks end? Ammunition boxes. Mortar carrier. They took on supplies there and then reversed into cover. I see one with its rear end peeking out near that warehouse."

Uncanny. Vasily grunted in mild approval, trying to mask his appreciation for the boy's sheer genius.

"Alright, we've found a support vehicle and maybe a command tank," he said. "Now let's map out the rest of their positions."

Petro tsked. "Aha. I see you," he announced. "Someone just lit a cigarette. There's a tight group of infantry sitting in the east of Mengshausen. Just off the road. Concealed in that - is that a school gymnasium? Now let's see. A decent commander would place something to the north with such a commanding view of the road. And yes! We have four Abrams tanks approximately one thousand meters. Right at the tree line. If you look closely enough, you can see the edges of the combat netting whipped up by the wind. There's the ambush. So where's the blocking force?"

"I see it. To the south. Right on 7," said Vasily. The squat vehicles sat right on the highway. The men on the road were moving around in broad daylight. It was unbelievable!

"No," said Petro. That's not it. "Those are engineers. They've mined the highway, and they apparently don't even care if we know it." He screwed on a 90mm zoom lens and snapped photo after photo.

Alen cursed in his own language and shook the field telephone's headset. "Dammit, I've lost contact with the BRDM. Stupid machine!"

The trees shook as the blades of a low-flying helicopter cut into the air around them. Alen nearly stood up. Vasily clamped a hand around the lieutenant's leg to stop him.

"Don't move!" he shouted.

The diminutive officer tumbled to the floor and landed with an angry yelp. He tried to struggle to get up, but Vasily pressed down on him with all his weight. "If you stand, I'll kill you!" he shouted.

The Huey shot up over the crest about four hundred meters to the south. It flew so low that the rotor wash rippled out along the tops of the pines. The door on the side was open. The machine gunner sat perched on the lip of the passenger bay. His legs were hooked over the edge of the machine with his feet planted on the skids. As the helicopter shot past, the wind whipped up the edges of Vasily's blanket. Soon, the green and brown patchwork cover was hurled over the side of the tower and floated toward the ground far below. Their cover was blown.

Vasily's heart sank as the helicopter circled back toward them.

"Go!" he shouted. "Run!"

He picked up Alen and tossed him at the staircase. His boy-like frame bounced off the railing and tumbled down the spiral staircase.

Petro wasted no time. He grabbed what little equipment he had brought and leaped over Alen's still form just as the first rounds of the American light machine gun sparked across the frame of the metal tower. Vasily followed, leaving the little Kazakhstani to his fate.

He cleared the fourth-floor stairs as the Huey drew back to a hover. The rounds punched through the air all around Vasily, who heard himself shouting and laughing like a maniac all the way down. On the third floor, he stepped over Petro's lifeless body.

The young man's limbs were sprawled out at awkward angles with the camera still slung around him. Vasily wrenched it off his dead friend's neck and continued his descent. Three awkward strides and he was over the little metal railing that wrapped around the second floor of the tower. Vasily had misjudged the height. When he finally hit, waves of pain shot through his legs. Just like he had been trained to do, he tucked his body and tumbled down the slope.

From somewhere behind him, the BRDM's engines grumbled and its wheels spun against the hard ground. The world slowed to a green and blue blur as Vasily's bumpy progress down the sloping ground to a halt. As he lay on the forest floor, the Huey lumbered toward the escaping BRDM-2. Pencil-thin machine gun tracers skipped off the top of the armored vehicle as it bumped along the rough path toward Vasily.

Seeing his chance, he took a deep breath and stood but immediately collapsed. Hot shards of agony sizzled in the space near his right calf muscles. The limb was broken. Another burst of machine gun fire tore into the earth as the BRDM-2 rolled closer. The idea of his body being crushed under the seven-ton weight of the oncoming vehicle's tires was enough to spur a second try.

He put all his weight on the remaining good leg and shoved off at the ground with both hands. For three long seconds, he stood on one foot and hopped while waving crazily at the fast-approaching scout vehicle. Fountains of dust kicked up all around him as the helicopter's machine gunner sprayed automatic fire down from treetop level. To Vasily's great relief, the BRDM jerked to a halt. The lower hatch on the right side of the vehicle's body creaked open. He hurled his body inside.

"Go! Go!" he screamed.

Vasily slid back and forth along the metal floor as the vehicle flew over rocks and skidded down the hill's steep slope. All the while, the clatter of the machine gun and the Huey stayed right along with them. Ivan veered hard left. Vasily sensed the whole vehicle about to tip over. When the BRDM settled back on the ground, the sound of rubber slapping against metal filled the vehicle's interior. Smoke wafted up from the instrument panel, obscuring Ivan's already limited view out the two square portholes.

Ivan slapped his hands against the beige metal dashboard. "We've got a flat! This is no damn good."

Vasily grunted and heaved his body into the gunner's seat. Through the periscope, he could see only the blur of the West German forest passing by. He rotated the turret with a hand crank until he finally caught sight of the Huey. A hundred meters to their rear, it chased after them like a hound to a fox.

He fired a long stream of 14.5 mm rounds at his pursuer. The tracers fell short of the Huey before Vasily corrected his aim and squeezed out another quick burst that tore chunks off the rotor head. The helicopter reeled back like a boxer dealt a sudden blow in the final round. A puff of dark smoke poured upward from the wounded beast. The BRDM rounded a sharp bend, throwing Vasily off the turret seat. His broken leg slammed into the back of the commander's seat sending a shuddering electric pain along his body. As he lay whimpering in the back of the scout car, Ivan glanced over at him.

"Well, that's one problem taken care of! Our friend is gone."

It was hard for Vasily to feel good. All he could do was reach into his little canvas bag and pull out the morphine vial. As it sunk into his thigh, the muscles unclenched. He floated the rest of the way home.

Half his team was dead, but he had Petro's camera and Alen's notes. Even if the Americans knew their ambush had been detected, it was too late to do anything about it. The attack would start soon enough. A faint smile descended as he drifted off to a dreamless sleep.

SOVIET PLAN OF ATTACK

CONCEALED
US TANKS + ATGMS

PLANNED
SOVIET
HE STRIKE

PLANNED
SOVIET
SMOKE
BARRAGE

Fulda

NIEDERAULA

OBJECTIVE
THREE

OBJECTIVE
TWO

MENGSHAUSEN

OB

Route 62

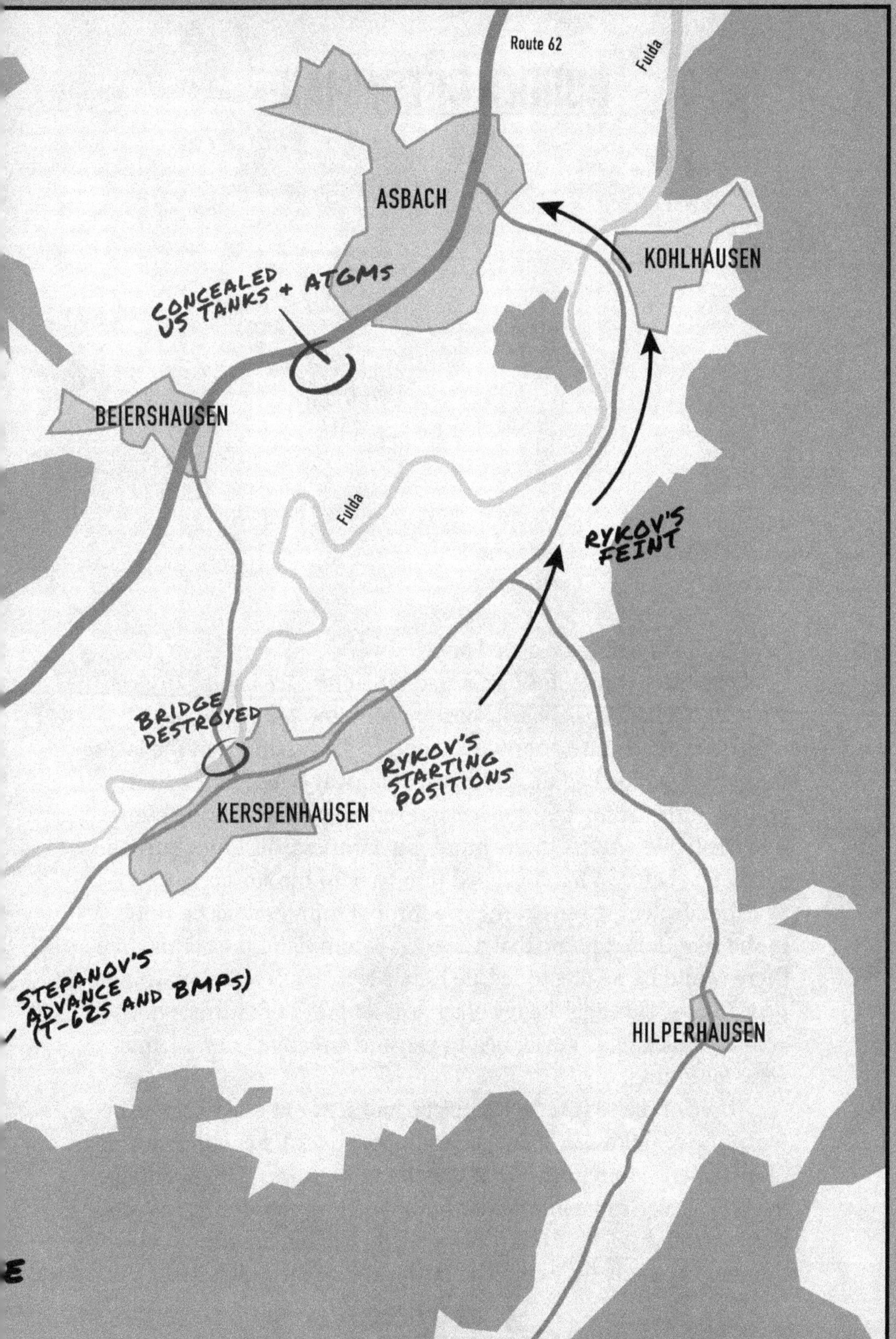

Route 62
Fulda
ASBACH
KOHLHAUSEN
CONCEALED
US TANKS + ATGMS
BEIERSHAUSEN
Fulda
RYKOV'S
FEINT
BRIDGE
DESTROYED
RYKOV'S
STARTING
POSITIONS
KERSPENHAUSEN
STEPANOV'S
ADVANCE
(T-62S AND BMPS)
HILPERHAUSEN

BURDEN OF COMMAND

Holzheim, West Germany
0640

Pavel had nearly drowned once.

One bitter winter, his father had taken him ice fishing in Prot-vino, a cold flat expanse just south of Moscow. Despite Pavel's reluctance to venture out on the smooth glassy surface of the lake, the elder Sokolov had urged him on. Halfway between the shore and the little fishing hut, the ice cracked open, and the boy plunged into the frigid waters. In the numbing darkness, his lungs burned in agony just before a hand yanked him back to the surface.

That drowning sensation bore through him now, as he stood in the abandoned home that served as a command post. This time there would be no one to rescue him. Major Pavel Sokolov would have to claw through the icy blackness and find the surface himself.

The attack hadn't even begun yet, and already the problems were mounting.

Three of the four recon teams he had sent out had not returned. Only one of them had managed to hobble back here with any kind of intelligence to report. What they had found was not encourag-ing. The American commander knew what he was doing. Instead of spreading his forces out piecemeal, he had apparently set up a number of deadly little traps on both sides of the Fulda River.

This complicated matters and forced him to make an uncomfortable choice.

Should he strike north or south?

On the west side of the river lay two towns - Asbach to the north and Niederaula to the south. He was ordered to take his battalion and capture at least one of them with all due speed. To the east of both villages lay a pair of narrow two-lane bridges, one of which he needed to take and hold. The route toward these bridges was guarded by mines and ambushes by infantry and tanks. Driving for both towns at the same time would result in the utter destruction of his forces. Even a less ambitious plan seemed impossible to pull off well enough.

If he went for the northern objective, his battalion would first need to capture the little town of Kohlhausen, which sat on the east bank of the Fulda River. Doing so would be no simple task. American infantry were huddled inside the little buildings and waiting for his tanks to roll down their narrow roads. Without infantry support, Pavel's armor would be slaughtered. Should he send along his infantry, they would easily be caught in a time-consuming battle in the streets.

But suppose his men succeeded.

Against all odds, maybe everything would go perfectly, and the town would be captured. His armored vehicles would then need to roll over the bridge and get ambushed by TOW vehicles concealed among the dug-in positions to the west. The tanks and carriers would be sitting ducks as they drove over the open fields on the way to Asbach. Battalion estimates had figured the casualty rate at an appalling sixty to eighty percent. Probably eighty.

The southern route held no greater appeal. On the east side of the Fulda River sat Mengshausen. As with Kohlhausen to the north, two platoons of American infantry were positioned in the town. He could try and bypass it by rushing around the hills to the east, but the American engineers had anticipated such a move and mined the entire route. He would have to send his men south down the road into the town. All the while, they would be exposed to defilade fire from the Abrams tanks that sat on the hillside to the northeast of Niederaula. The losses would be devastating.

A gust of wind blew through the smashed window, and Pavel slapped the map to keep it from blowing away. Its edges fluttered like a trapped butterfly. Major Ulmanis walked over to him with a hot glass of tea and set it on the dusty kitchen table. Pavel nodded thanks and reached out as if he were going under for the third time.

"Major, I - I could use some advice. If you're not too busy, that is."

The blond Latvian shrugged. "Very well."

Pavel gestured toward the wooden chair and swept away the chunks of plaster on the table. Ulmanis sat there with a face unperturbed by the prospect of coming battle. How could he remain so calm at a time like this?

"Well, I want to know what you think of the current situation," said Pavel. "You've seen the same reports and the briefings. Do we go north or south?"

Ulmanis' eyes danced with an answer, but his mouth remained shut. The ice between them needed to be smashed, but Pavel wasn't sure how. The man seemed to revel in being aloof and standoffish. He was always notably absent at the political officer's lectures. He rarely showed up to the regimental functions, and when he did, he arrived late and left early. Pavel had never seen the man drunk nor even drink. He was the battalion's shadow - always in the background, saying nothing and quietly carrying out his orders to the letter.

Ulmanis had been the battalion executive officer for five solid years. Because of that, he understood the men and knew their capabilities. Pavel, by contrast, had been field promoted from company to battalion commander at the behest of his high-ranking father. Pavel's leapfrog in rank and responsibility had caused none of the expected resentment from Ulmanis. Instead, the man had merely shrugged and accepted the situation. Now Pavel was in over his head, and Ulmanis was his only lifeline. It was time to reach out and ask for help. It was either that or face a firing squad.

Pavel jarred his brain and tried to think of a way to forge some quick bond with this man. The only connection he shared with him was a brief stay in his hometown of Riga. Six months of high school had resulted in a shaky grasp of Latvian, but it would have to do.

The foreign words stumbled out of Pavel's mouth. He murdered his participles and wounded the consonants. His verbs were left unconjugated. The sentences staggered out of his mouth like a lush at closing time. It had been twelve years since he had uttered a word of the language. The effort he now made was the product of his father's brief military posting in the Baltic republic. From the bewildered expression on Ulmanis' face, Pavel had the sense that he was speaking like a caveman. It was not long before he felt like an idiot for the attempt.

The edges of the major's frown inched upward. His cold eyes flickered with life as they roamed Pavel's face.

"You know, I don't understand a damn word you just said," Ulmanis confessed. "But you tried. Someday I might teach you. Let's stick to Russian for now."

A little victory. Ulmanis leaned over and rested a hand on the dusty table.

"You are under the impression that one of these two routes is better than the other, but you don't know why. The answer is you can't know why and you will only find out by sending your men there to die. That's the truth of it. A good commander will go by intuition. A great commander will find reasons for his decision after luck reveals its hand. What you must do is to remember the first basic principle of operations - consider your advantages. You have three companies of men and three companies of tanks. That means there are lives to spend to ensure the outcome is favorable."

Pavel tried to parse out the meaning of the words, but they were coming at him from obtuse angles.

"You are telling me to drive the attack on both objectives?"

Ulmanis shook his head slowly. "No. You are right that one is better than two but not because your men cannot do it. It is because simple is always better than complex."

"If I drive for the southern objective, do you think we will make it?"

Ulmanis ran a hand over the map and leafed through the razvedka photographs. He smoothed his mustache and spoke.

"You will be caught in a trap. The American commander will send his forces down from the north to reinforce Niederaula.

The men will die before they reach the objective."

The room spun in circles of despair. "So it is hopeless!"

"You are not listening," said Ulmanis. "You must prevent those American reinforcements from arriving. Make a convincing feint toward the northern objective at the right time."

"How will I know when that comes?"

Ulmanis lit a cigarillo and sipped at his tea. He seemed pacific in the way he crossed his legs and looked on like a great grandfather watching his children play in the backyard. After a long moment of staring into space, he nodded. "Let me take care of that, Pavel Sokolov."

MAELSTROM

Captain Mikhail Stepanov opened the hatch of his T-62 tank and smiled as the diesel-stained air swept into his dirty lungs. After four hours of sitting in the tank's belly, the attack signal had finally come. Three shrill blasts of his whistle spurred the long column of armored vehicles west towards the Fulda River. So far things had gone smoothly. None of the aging tanks had suffered a mechanical failure, and the skies above had remained mercifully clear of enemy planes or helicopters. Stepanov marveled at how everything had been so easy and light, almost like a field exercise.

The low hills to the west masked their progress from the line of departure. Soon his men would meet the flat open road that would take them south to his first objective, the town of Mengshausen. If they ventured forth, the company would be cut to pieces by a pair of Abrams tanks positioned a kilometer east of here. Major Sokolov, the battalion commander, had circled them in red on the map. He had even taken the time to show Stepanov the grainy reconnaissance photos. Two big hulking American beasts sat near the treeline close to the final objective, Niederaula.

Stepanov checked the company's mapbook and read off the coordinates to himself as the tanks under his command halted again. He breathed a single codeword into the radio and waited for the nightmare to begin. Soon, the American tank position would be blanketed with high explosive artillery shells.

A smoke barrage along the west bank of the river would obscure his company's movement. Although the enemy had thermal sights that could "see" through the standard chemicals used to generate such smoke, Stepanov had been assured that some unknown substance - possibly graphite - had been mixed into the batch. This ingredient would confuse the fire control system of the tanks for a short time.

If that were true, his tanks would charge like horse cavalry all the way to their objective in Mengshausen without so much as a scratch. The squat BMP infantry fighting vehicles behind them would enter the town and unload their steel bellies full of infantry. When the brave Red Army soldiers killed every American defender, they would charge west over the river again and do the same in Niederaula. And that would be that! The battle would be over and, with any luck, his company would have inched along the map enough for one morning.

The shriek of artillery rounds consumed the air.

Stepanov balled his hands into fists. A series of dull thumps drummed against the ground on the eastern river bank. His heart fell as he realized the smoke rounds were landing two hundred meters off-target. Thick gray clouds welled up two hundred meters away from his tank. The wind kicked up at the same moment, and a wall of fog swept towards his position. He and the rest of the company were engulfed by the gloomy soup. Stepanov couldn't see more than a few meters around him.

He expected to hear the high explosive land far to the west, but the thunder did not come. Thirty seconds passed, and nothing happened.

Stepanov heard his own voice shake in anger as he spoke over the radio net.

COMPANY THREE TO MAIN. WHERE IS THE HIGH EXPLOSIVE? THERE IS ONLY SMOKE, OVER.

The radio bleated like a dying sheep back at him. The jamming had been bad enough all morning, but the high intervening hill between his company and the battalion headquarters proved to be too much of an obstacle. A garbled transmission came back a few moments later, but Stepanov wasn't even sure if it was in reply.

If the high explosive rounds didn't arrive soon, the smoke would dissipate, and he would lose his cover. It was time to move. He would have to trust that the smoke would be enough to protect his tanks from the enemy guns.

Stepanov blew into the whistle with all his might. The roar of diesel engines welled up behind him. Stepanov strained to hear the groan of explosions to the east, still hoping that the high explosive shells would arrive. Still nothing.

His tank driver accelerated through the gray cotton-like mass that swirled around them. Inside the smoke cloud, the bright morning sun appeared little more than a hint of bronze. The rest of the world took on a corpse-like pallor. Stepanov's universe collapsed to a few meters distance on either side of the hull. From where he stood, he could just barely make out the rear fuel drums of the tank to his front. Of the tank behind him, only the very tip of the main gun's long barrel could be seen.

"I can't see!" shouted the driver.

Stepanov ducked down into the tank. "Drive! Just drive as fast as you can. Do not stop."

The cloud flickered with light from somewhere ahead, and a bone-shaking wallop washed over Stepanov. The screech of metal on metal grew louder as the tank drove on. The captain's hands shot up around his ears. Like a thousand nails on a chalkboard, the clangor overwhelmed all rational thought.

Soon they passed by the shattered remnants of the lead T-62. The egg-shaped turret had been dissected from the hull with clinical efficiency. A short pillar of flame erupted from the turret ring. The next tank behind it had followed too close and driven straight into it at 50 kilometers per hour. Now its treads and main gun were somehow entangled in the wreckage.

Stepanov's tank continued along the edge of the pavement. Something loud and deadly and unforgiving happened behind him. Men screamed and died somewhere nearby, but he couldn't see them. The shrieks subsided behind him as the T-62 drove onward. His relief was cut short by a metallic punch and explosive clatter that marked the end of another tank. One by one, his tanks were being picked apart by the American gunners.

The smoke either did not work as well as he had been told or it was a complete lie. Either way, they had been betrayed. Hot shards of anger dug into his brain.

He keyed the radio to the company net and spoke.

ALL TANKS RETURN FIRE! DON'T JUST DRIVE. SHOOT!

A panicky voice shot out over the static.

WE CAN'T SEE ANYTHING! THERE'S NOTHING TO SHOOT!

It was Lieutenant Bukin, the sniveling little brat who thumped his chest during this morning's briefing. Stepanov savored the terror in his tone.

TURN YOUR TURRET NINETY DEGREES RIGHT AND FIRE. I DON'T CARE IF YOU CAN'T SEE AN ENEMY TANK. YOU WILL SHOOT AND KEEP SHOOTING UNTIL WE REACH THE OBJECTIVE, OVER.

A pair of main guns bellowed behind him in the swirling vortex.

Captain Stepanov wiped a gloved hand across his grease-smeared face and tried to hold back the urge to vomit. It was hopeless but what else could he do?

The T-62's infrared sights were effective only at short ranges. The idea of hitting anything at all was laughable. His own tank's weapon blared uselessly. Stepanov took heart as he listened to the ebb of panic in his crew's voices. Perhaps even the illusion of fighting back was enough to quell the terror.

Stepanov stopped counting after his tank drove past the fifth destroyed T-62. There was nothing to do about it other than to keep pushing onward through the smoke and fire and death of this first morning of the war. The eye-watering exhaust and the ear-splitting volume of nearby tank fire had forced him back into the belly of his tank. Any romantic notions of war were laid to rest when he noticed the body of his executive officer lying on the ground next to his tank. The man's stomach had been split wide open. He screamed like a demon hurled over the abyss. Stepanov's tank rumbled on.

The map meant nothing. He was completely disoriented and blind. A quick check of a handheld compass confirmed they were heading south, but Stepanov had no idea how far they were from Mengshausen. For all he knew, they could have passed right through it. He asked Bebchuk, the driver, but all he got in response was a half-hearted guess that they were "probably very close" to the objective. The tank was off the road now. Stepanov had ordered his men to stay off because too many of his tanks had to swerve around the wreckage of other vehicles. Now and again, he caught sight of a dark outline of a T-62 rushing beside his vehicle or coming up from behind. Then they would disappear back into the fog like some sort of old ghost ship.

It was only when Stepanov's tank passed yet another flaming metal wreck that he was able to discern the outlines of single-story buildings and farmhouses that characterized the town. The smoke thinned out just enough near the edges of the town to allow the dull hues of greens and blues to pierce the iron cocoon that surrounded him.

At long last, daylight lunged into his narrowed eyes. He dared to turn his gaze back upon the long trail of wreckage strewn on the road. Blinking back tears, he could only mutter two words at the devastation wrought upon his men.

"My God…"

At 0645, Company Three of the Third Battalion had begun the day's fighting with thirteen T-62 tanks.

By 0648, only three remained.

HAIR TRIGGER

Mengshausen, West Germany
0650

Private Vanya Samokhin sat in the passenger compartment of the BMP and retched as each cold wave of terror washed over him. Through the firing ports that lined the vehicle's interior walls, the burning tanks and mangled bodies rolled past like a horror show. Despite all his wishes, he could not get up and leave. He was trapped in here with the other men in his squad.

Somewhere out there, the enemy was lashing out at them with leisurely cruelty. If he had believed in any God, he would have prayed. Instead, he squeezed his eyes shut and lied to himself that he would somehow survive this ordeal. As if in mockery, another explosion ripped through the air.

Finally, the cloud of smoke thinned and dissolved. Vanya felt like a feeble imitation of a stage magician making his dramatic entrance.

Their BMP halted as a hard metal rain of small arms fire poured down on its outer shell.

Lieutenant Ovechkin screamed out in a hoarse rage-filled voice. "Fire!"

Along with the other soldiers on the hull-facing bench, Vanya lunged forward and shoved the barrel of his AKM assault rifle into the port across from him. Not ten feet away from where he sat flashed the muzzles of two or three figures firing from behind sandbags. Most of the rounds skipped off the side of the fighting vehicle with a series of ping ping pings, but the man beside him slid face-first to the floor and bled out among the spare ammunition crates. Vanya gulped out a warning when one of the men in the shop stood up with a tube-like device in his hands. He was blond and tall and thin - the first American he had ever seen in his life.

Vanya yanked the trigger. His weapon jumped back against his shoulder as it joined the fusillade of all the other rifles in his squad. In a mere handful of seconds, the jerking recoil halted. A few panicky breaths later, he had found the source of the problem. The magazine was bone dry. Vanya reached down with trembling fingers and fumbled to remove a new one from the pouch on his combat webbing. He had no idea if he had hit anything and no time to wonder about it.

The BMP's engine coughed before it accelerated down the rubble-strewn street. The constant rattle of small arms derailed even the simplest of thoughts. Parts of Vanya shook and trembled, and he felt as if he might explode at any moment. There was only so much he could do - only so many things he could tell himself to keep the terror under control.

Ovechkin screeched an order. The rear doors swung open.

The BMP kept crawling forward as the men spilled from the vehicle. Vanya was the last one out. He entered a world set to maximum volume and brightness. His right boot caught on something soft. He tumbled to the broken pavement. An unceasing storm of weapons fire swept all around him. Tracers leaped from building windows while the flash of grenades lit up the interior of nearby buildings.

One of the T-62s further down the street belted out a tank round. The walls of a beautiful home blasted outward. Chunks of brick and mortar tumbled to the sidewalk. To his right, a soldier shouted through a blood-drenched face for help. A desperate hand flung out toward Vanya, who recoiled in horror.

"Nononono!" he shouted back at the thing.

In an effort to get away, Vanya scrambled to his feet. The rest of his squad sat crouched with their backs to the wall of a windowless concrete building. Ovechkin beckoned him over. Vanya's legs pumped as if he were caught in a bad dream.

The lieutenant screamed over the din of automatic weapon fire.

"We take this building at all costs!" he shouted. "Prepare to move."

Vanya peered upward and understood the reason for the assault. Enemy machine gun fire and rocket rounds spat out from the top of the structure. Soviet infantrymen crumpled like paper as they emerged from the back of a BMP down the street. Tracers whizzed down from the top of the tall building and sliced into the group of men as they tried in vain to disperse into the road. Vanya pictured the Americans on the rooftop as they hurled gore and death at a whim. To a man, they were sharp-toothed demons who laughed maniacally at the suffering they caused.

The squad charged toward the metal door near one corner of the building. Two men swung the butts of their rifles at its hard surface. After several bone-shaking knocks, one of the weapons shattered.

Ovechkin shoved his way through the crowd and demanded a grenade from each squad member. When a dozen of the explosives were collected, he wrapped them together with a boot lace from some unlucky corporal. The entire bulky apparatus was set in front of the door. Vanya scattered back towards the street and crouched behind the twisted remains of a bench. Ovechkin pulled the pin on one of the grenades and sprinted toward the corpse of a box-shaped car buried under a heap of rubble.

When Vanya looked back at the stubborn gymnasium door, it was already gone. Smoke belched from the blackened doorframe. Ovechkin scrambled over the roof of the car and gave off three shrill bleats of his whistle. The squad bolted towards the doorway. Vanya plucked up the courage to run along with the others.

Enveloped by fear, his view of the world took on a grainy slow-motion quality.

Two men ran straight over the threshold, only to be met with a thick stream of gunfire that drilled into their torsos and upper bodies. Only a heartbeat ago, they were Constantin and Arkady. Now they were just a heap of torn meat covered in blood and dust.

Ovechkin stood by the wall next to the opening and tossed in a pair of smoke grenades. A cloud billowed out of the hole. Three sharp whistle blasts sent the other men surging forward into the heavy plume. Vanya steeled himself and plunged into the waiting darkness. The world he entered rang with guttural screams and the snap of rifle fire. His senses gave up on trying to guess what was happening all around him. He found himself crawling along the hard rubber floor and calling out his mother's name again and again.

The smoke in the room soon dissipated, revealing hints of the misery all around him. A foggy tendril would lift just enough from the floor. A mangled comrade lay there with a bayonet sticking straight up out his chest like a flagpole. The smoke would draw back in again.

Something gripped his shoulder. A torrent of foreign words flooded out. Propelled by terror, Vanya lashed out with his rifle. The bayonet at the end slid into soft flesh. Just as he had been taught, he twisted the rifle and pulled it out. He did it again and again until he could do it no more.

With great heaping gulps of breath, Vanya rested as the smoke wafted up into the high rafters just as the last of the firing and shouting and killing finally came. He found himself kneeling in the middle of the painted wooden floor. Yesterday, children laughed and played and ran here with their teachers for the last time. Today, it was covered in bodies and slick with blood.

Who had won this little battle? That was obvious. No one. Vanya felt something seep through his chest. It was as if the last remnants of his own childhood had been torn away from him. For the rest of his life, he knew there would be nothing left for him. No possible good could live in the cold heavy stillness that was nestled deep inside.

"Let's go!" someone shouted. It was Lieutenant Ovechkin, the only other man in this vast room who was still alive.

Vanya did as he was told. Over the bodies and collapsed sandbags, he stepped and weaved until he found the staircase that led up to the roof. When they got to the door, Ovechkin gave a hand signal and kicked it open. Vanya stepped out into the sunlight. Across from him, close to the rooftop's edge, were three Americans. Two of them fired rockets down into the street below. The other reached into one of the nearby crates and handed a new launcher to each man. None of them turned to see Vanya. He brought the rifle up and squeezed out a series of quick bursts. The Americans crumpled like paper.

Vanya reloaded and sat down on the flat expanse. To the north sat a long string of burning T-62 tanks. Over to the west lay another town on the other side of the nearby river. He had no doubt they would go there next. None of this death and killing would stop until either the Americans were defeated or he was killed. The idea of going home seemed like a sick joke.

Ovechkin returned some time later with the remnants of Second and Third Squad. On Vanya's rooftop, the lieutenant put each man to work setting up Saggers and searching for targets near the sweeping hills that rose up on the west bank of the river. Someone spotted a tank and in a tone that betrayed no excitement, its location was announced and the distance estimated. Vanya stepped back, careful not to get caught in the fiery backblast of the launch.

At last, the pair of wire-guided anti-tank missiles whipped out. A few seconds later, one of the men chuckled, and the mood lightened. Someone smacked Vanya on the back.

"Yuri just knocked out an American tank! Look!"

Vanya peered through the binoculars. Sure enough, the crippled beast burned amid a copse of trees halfway up the long gentle slope of a massive hill. He took no joy in it. Only a chilly sense of satisfaction.

THE PRODIGAL SON

Pavel stumbled out of the house and stretched his limbs before lighting a celebratory cigarette. His battalion had just captured the first objective. Though losses had been reported as "heavy," a pair of on-scene commanders had apprised him of the venture's progress. The first report had merely stated that Mengshausen was being cleared. A few minutes later, a lieutenant breathlessly informed him that the US presence in Mengshausen had been "wiped out." Anti-tank missiles were now hitting American defenses across the river.

It was excellent news, but the battle was far from decided. War had its own way of throwing hot flaming obstacles at you every step of the way. The battle's very start had perfectly demonstrated this principle.

When the opening barrage failed to arrive as promised, Pavel had wasted precious minutes on the radio trying to determine what had gone wrong. Finally, an artillery sergeant informed him that the self-propelled guns on the ridge behind him were being systematically blown to pieces by a low-flying American plane. The air defenses for the regimental artillery were caught in a traffic jam about ten kilometers to the rear. The carnage only stopped after the blasted aircraft had delivered its entire load of ordnance and turned for home.

By that time, the damage was done. When he finally focused his attention back to the progress of the operation, Stepanov's T-62's were being shot to pieces on a death ride south to the first objective. For three lonely minutes, Pavel sat there across from Major Ulmanis in solemn silence, waiting for any news of what had happened. When the time elapsed and still no word had come back, Pavel had argued that he should send out a runner to pull back whatever remained of the company and regroup it into a reserve. The executive officer declared the decision "rash" and urged him to wait another three minutes. With his knees knocking and fists clenched, Pavel stared at the radio as each grueling second ticked by.

The next radio reports from Stepanov came from within the town itself. They had made it. Barely.

One of Pavel's aides slipped out the back door and stood at attention. The corporal's face bulged with strain as he spoke in a fatigued and almost surly tone.

"Sir. Our infantry has seized the bridge over the Fulda. You wanted to be informed."

Pavel crumpled the flaming butt under his boot and walked back inside without a word.

Ulmanis stood at the long table in the middle of the room, shuffling the reports on the desk into neat piles.

Pavel clapped his hands as he approached. "So it seems we captured a bridge!"

Ulmanis didn't look up. "I shouldn't be here. Two commanders in the same place. It's dangerous."

"I need you here."

"Not anymore, Pavel. You need a subordinate out in the field to help push through your commands."

"But -."

Ulmanis stood. "With your permission, sir. I will go out and prepare Third Company for the final stage of the operation."

And so the time had come. It was time for the feint that would keep the Americans pinned down to the north while the infantry groped toward victory in the south.

The weight of responsibility crushed down on Pavel's shoulders as Ulmanis slipped on a helmet and strode out to his command BMP.

An aide clapped his feet together and tilted his chin towards the bank of radios and monitors that lined the entire south wall of the command post.

"Sir, we have incoming radio reports. Our forces in Mengshausen are ready for the final attack toward Niederaula. What shall we do?"

Now it was time for the sacrifice. All forces would be committed. An entire company would be sacrificed in the service of victory. He hesitated at the thought of sending so many men to their death. Surely, there must be a better way. He would wait for clear indications from his men that the time was ripe. Surely another ten minutes of consolidating their progress wouldn't hurt.

"Tell all companies to hold," he said.

The radio operator's face twisted as the words sunk in.

"But, sir - we have already received word that the southern group is ready to attack."

Pavel slapped the desk. Sheets of paper scattered to the floor like snow.

"I told you to order them to wait!"

DRIVE ON NIEDERAULA

Major Ulmanis' command BMP rolled along the smooth roads that led to Rykov's company. When he arrived, three platoons of infantry carriers were sitting there in a long column along the road east of Kohlhausen. The dismounted infantry stood outside their carriers, smoking and chatting with each other as if they were on an exercise. An angry fire swept up in his belly as he looked on in disbelief.

Ulmanis disapproved of what he was about to do. He found displays of emotion distasteful. That he was now being forced to make one added fuel to his disgust. He slid down from the turret and landed on the ground at a trot. As he ran past the clumps of men, he screamed out.

"Get back in your vehicles or I'll have each of you shot!"

The effect was electric. Butts were flung and dashed underfoot. Hatches slid open and closed.

Captain Rykov popped up in the cupola of his command vehicle. His eyes went wide as saucers with Ulmanis' approach. The company commander held up his hands as if he were about to receive a blow.

"Sir, we were just waiting as order-," he said.

"Idiot! Get your men moving now!"

Without further ado, the engines of his vehicles roared.

Major Ulmanis planted a boot on Rykov's BMP and climbed up. He yanked Rykov by the chin straps of his helmet. In a tired blustery rage, he screamed.

"Once you reach Kohlhausen, do not stop! Move west across the bridge and go straight for Asbach. Speed, captain! Do you understand?"

Rykov screamed back like a recruit on his first day of training. "Yes, sir!"

Ulmanis jumped down from the BMP and waved his arms like a madman. The long column of vehicles slithered by as the exhaust churned in the wind. The stench of diesel fumes bit at his brain. He nearly smiled until he glanced over at Rykov's vehicle. The captain stared back in Ulmanis' direction. From the forlorn expression on his face, the man must have sensed that his company was the sacrificial lamb for the rest of the battalion.

So be it.

All Rykov's men needed to do was survive just long enough to distract the Americans near Asbach. If that happened, there was at least an even chance that the southern objective could be taken. If it failed, he would send a thousand more like Rykov to their doom. That was fine. War, as he understood it, was a battle of will just as much as it was about training and equipment. If officers like the soft Sokolov did not have the heart to do what was needed, then the whole cursed task would fall to men who were strong enough to shoulder the burden of churning out entire oceans of widows and orphans. This could not be done from the sterile atmosphere of a command center.

Ulmanis' BMP crawled south alongside the road that led to Mengshausen. The pavement was littered with the burnt-out crusts of Stepanov's tanks. Some of them still sat there with their ammunition cooking off, exploding again and again. Ulmanis didn't need to urge the driver to give the dying vehicles a wide berth.

Through the haze, he caught a glimpse of the events further south. While a small force of men and vehicles stayed behind in the town of Mengshausen to provide cover fire, a handful of tanks and a half-dozen BMPs lunged straight west over the bridge and into the fields just east of Niederaula.

Fifty meters beyond the west bank, the roadside detonated in a hail of dirt and fire. The nearest T-62 halted, and smoke drizzled out of its hatches. Another tank crunched to a halt as the ground underneath it flung out a blackened mix of debris and soil.

Ulmanis understood the problem right away. The lead tanks were stuck in a minefield. Behind them, the BMPs stalled to a halt as the deadly dilemma dawned upon them. Go forward and die soon. Stay and die later.

The slap bang of a tank gun to the west and the almost immediate evisceration of a BMP revealed the true extent of the peril. The southern offensive was now bogged down. Defeat was in their grasp. Something needed to be done or it was finished. Ulmanis rattled off a quick situation report to Sokolov and then simply ignored the confused responses. There was no time left to play on the radio. He coaxed the BMP's driver to drive south and cross over the bridge to join the deadly morass. His command vehicle passed close to a burning tank, and he winced as the searing heat bit at his flesh.

"Stay off the road!" he commanded his BMP driver. "Get into the fields! Do not stop!"

The ground behind him rolled like a wave under the impact of incoming tank rounds. Ulmanis kept one hand wrapped around a small metal handle just under the commander's hatch. It was all he could do to keep from pitching head-first out of the bucking BMP. Every instant he was still alive seemed a miracle. At any second, he fully expected to hear an explosion from underneath the vehicle and that would be it. Instead, the little vehicle bounded forward over the uncultivated earth.

Ulmanis waved his arms to get the attention of the vehicle commanders as he passed. Their heads tracked him as if he were some kind of terrible demon urging them on through the gates of Hell. Sure enough, a trickle of BMPs and tanks surged west in loose formation. The tanks in front formed a crooked wedge and returned volleys of fire at the American defensive positions near the town. One of the carriers near the rear struck a mine and flipped on its side, but the others kept driving.

Ulmanis clutched the map in one hand and called in grid co-ordinates. When asked for a fire mission code, he dropped the list down into the BMP.

"Just hit them with everything. All of it!"

Would the artillery come? It didn't matter. Momentum was building now. Another turn of the radio dial and he was soon talking in clipped phrases to Lieutenant Ovechkin, who had assumed command of the covering force in Mengshausen.

"Get everyone over here. Move as fast as you can!"

The first round splashed down five hundred meters straight ahead in the center of Niederaula. A tall fountain of fire and rock and trees blew sky-high. A freight train cut the air above his head, and a row of buildings that ran along the outskirts of the town was smothered in sheer destructive power. When the smoke cleared, much of the place was just a memory of better times. Ulmanis' throat clutched at the air, hot and thick with soot and ash. He covered his mouth and nose with a sleeve as the group of vehicles slowed.

When the tremors finally ceased five full minutes later, half the town of Niederaula had disappeared. A quiet descended over the battlefield. Somewhere in the rubble, a dazed American soldier walked around in lazy circles.

Ulmanis prodded the driver with a foot to continue on. His vehicle surged forward in the lead. Halfway to the torn-up remnants of the town, the vehicle suddenly stopped. A wretched pain shot up into his legs. Ulmanis ducked down to find the entire crew compartment smothered in black smoke. The driver leaned forward over the controls, not moving at all. Ulmanis didn't bother checking his own wounds. His legs burned and the entire lower half of his fatigues were mere shreds. Soon his legs gave out entirely, and only the small metal handle near his waist kept him from falling down into the burning compartment.

Using every ounce of strength to stand in the cupola, he waved the tanks and BMPs onward across the field and into the town. As they passed by, some of the men stared back at him. One of them snapped off a salute.

When they had all passed him by, Ulmanis dropped down into the belly of his command BMP, the heat and smoke dragging him to a dark place from which he would never return.

AFTERMATH

The reports flooded in and Pavel said nothing. Without Ulmanis to guide him, he was unable to make much sense of what he heard. Some of it was contradictory while others were obviously wrong. Without someone on his staff who could effectively filter it out for him, each morsel of information had the same weight. Ulmanis had told him most of being an effective leader was about building a mental picture of what was happening and acting accordingly. Easy to say but nearly impossible to do without experience and mentoring. Since his executive officer had left ten minutes ago, he possessed neither. Things were happening not because of his leadership but despite it.

"Sir, we have reports from the southern group," said the battalion intelligence officer. He was a wiry lieutenant who would have been right at home working in a factory office near Minsk. His beady eyes fell to the floor as if he were expecting some kind of question. Pavel knew he should ask something, but what? Unable to muster the energy to dig further into his brain, he simply threw up a hand.

The lieutenant coughed and continued. "The town of Niederaula is now liberated thanks to their - and your - efforts. The final objective has been seized."

"What about Rykov's men?"

A pause.

"Sir, no word from Rykov yet…but - as I mentioned earlier - they came under heavy fire from American tanks and vehicles near Asbach. Since then, there have been no transmissions."

The gears whirred in Pavel's brain. So Rykov had advanced on Asbach and died for it. Who was responsible for that?

"What remains of our forces in the south?"

"A proper accounting has still not been done yet, sir," said the lieutenant. "But from what we can gather at this time, we currently have one T-62 tank and four active BMPs."

Pavel took a deep breath. Was he really hearing this? An hour ago, there were hundreds of men and dozens of machines under his command. Now, he had about a platoon's worth of them left. The true extent of this horrible victory came peeled off one question at a time.

Pavel croaked out the next word. "Casualties."

"Again, too early to give definite numbers but we can safely presume that casualties are very heavy. A makeshift hospital has already been set up in Mengshausen."

He watched the lieutenant as he gave this news. The man's eyes were furtive and his voice a blank. The urge welled up within Pavel to lunge over and grab the man by the throat. He was being protected again. But this time, it was not his father doing it. It was his own men.

"Numbers!" he said, shocked by the darkness of the words. The lieutenant's face twisted just enough. A morsel of contempt and fear. The exact same faces that Pavel had made at his father.

The lieutenant flipped through a thick pad of papers and spoke without lifting his head. "Initial estimates are approximately sixty dead and one hundred wounded, many of them serious.

The quiet astonishment was filled with the shrill ring of a telephone on Pavel's desk. His hand swung down and gripped the receiver. The words of the divisional commander crackled through. "Major Sokolov, I hear that your battalion has won the day over at Niederaula. Excellent work. Regroup your forces and prepare to drive west again. Do it quickly!" The line clicked over.

Pavel smoothed his tunic and set the receiver down. Over the heaps of corpses of his men, he had achieved a victory, and now this was what it felt like. It was at this moment, he could choose to let the weight bear down on him and destroy him. Nothing would change. He would be shuttled off to a new appointment. A replacement for him would be chosen. The machine would march on, killing and dying and suffering the whole way. Pavel studied the lined face of his father in the old photograph that sat perched on the edge of his desk.

He clapped his hands together twice and threw his voice over the beeps and clicks of machinery that filled the command post. The eyes of his staff turned toward him.

"Orders have come down from division. I want all efforts aimed at bringing the battalion back to combat-level readiness. Logistics will provide a detailed account of all necessary reinforcements and supplies needed. I want this battalion ready to advance in one hour. Am I understood?!"

US PLAN OF ATTACK

PLANNED US HE STRIKE

Fulda

HEMMEN

X

OBJECTIVE KNIGHT

SOVIET DEFENSIVE POSITIONS

FOX'S ADVANCE (COSTA)

DELTA'S ADVANCE (HARLAND)

HARRIS ADVANCE

LÜDERMÜND

OBJECTIVE ROOK

Fulda

DUG-IN SOVIET TROOPS

X

PLANNED US SMOKE BARRAGE

Fulda

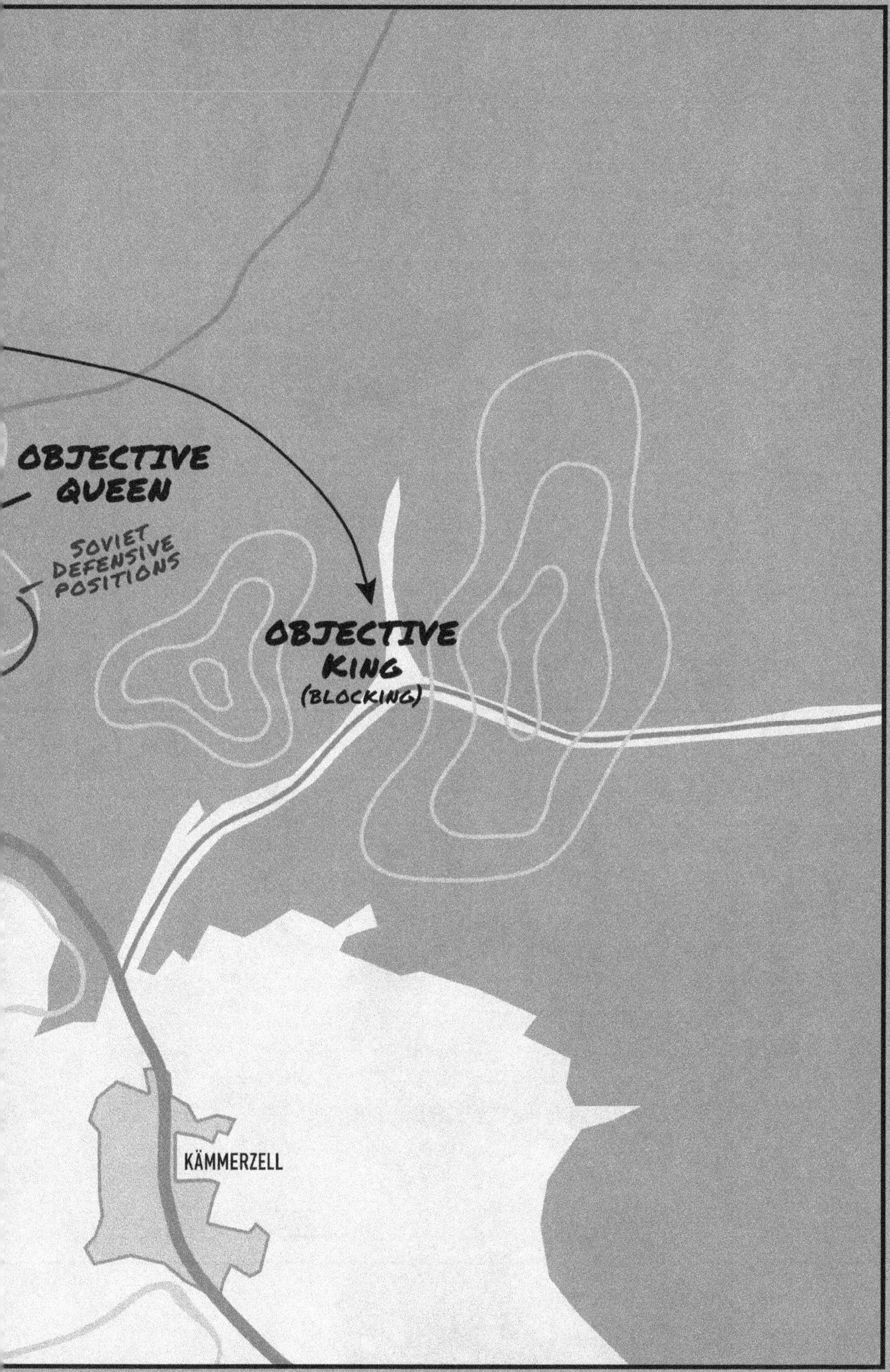

OBJECTIVE QUEEN
SOVIET DEFENSIVE POSITIONS
OBJECTIVE KING (BLOCKING)
KÄMMERZELL

HARD CHOICES

Colonel Ted Mackinsky picked up the stack of photographs on his desk and sifted through them once again. He just had to be sure.

The first shot showed a T-55 tank in the middle of a suburban street. Captured frozen at the edges of the frame were three figures in mid-stride. The guy in the lead wore a pair of blue jeans and a sweater that would have made Cliff Huxtable proud. Definitely not Territorialheer. A few yards behind him was a woman with long hair and a pleated skirt. Her mouth was twisted in panic and her eyes wide with anguish. Bringing up the rear was a girl in a school uniform.

The rest of the photos were variations on the same theme.

Amid the hundreds of pictures of Fulda snapped by the 11th Armored Cavalry scouts, the evidence was overwhelming. The Soviets were in the city, and the West German inhabitants were trapped there with them. As the leader of Task Force Lance, he had pinned his hopes on a quick battalion-sized counterattack to reclaim a few bridges that the Soviets had taken early on in their offensive. With this newest batch of intelligence, it was clear that completing such a task would surely leave thousands of innocents dead.

"How many people are we talking about here?" asked Mackinsky.

Major Clifton shook his head. "We don't have exact numbers, sir. But the pre-war population was around forty thousand people."

Mackinsky dropped the stack of photos and shoved them away in disgust. He wanted to scream at the intelligence officer, but that would just be killing the messenger.

"What if we move around their flanks? Make a surprise attack. No bombardment. Just run in and catch them with their pants down?"

"Sir, you'd be facing dug-in infantry supported by tanks," said Clifton. "If you go in there without artillery support-."

Mackinsky bristled. "I know that! But think of the West Germans. The political reaction will be dynamite. We drop a hundred tons of TNT into Fulda, and it'll drive Bonn straight towards the bargaining table."

Cifton didn't answer. Instead, he just stood up and paced around the room. His face was a sheen of exhaustion and sweat and fatigue. Mackinsky felt guilty and tried to think of something to say to console the man, but nothing came. When General Basevi, the commander of US V Corps, had tasked him with finding a suitable place for a counterattack, Mackinsky had set Clifton up with the job of coordinating the intelligence collection efforts to locate potential targets.

The man had moved bureaucratic mountains and ruffled more than a few feathers to bring as many of NATO's precious few resources to bear. Scouts were dispatched. RF-4 reconnaissance aircraft were launched. Even a few of the new Lockheed drones were brought out of testing and flown over the shattered landscape to take photo after photo. The result had been a goldmine of intelligence.

Mackinsky had initially been overjoyed by the results. Of the three potential targets for a counterattack, Fulda was the most attractive due to its proximity to the 8th Infantry Division along with the lack of any serious Soviet presence in the area. The battalions that sat there now were from the 247th Guards Motorized Rifle Regiment, which consisted of aging hardware like T-55s and T-62s.

In his mind, the colonel could see the battle go his way already. Two companies from the 8th ID and a squadron from 2/11 ACR would do the job. The ACR scouts would pick out and identify targets. Then Delta Company's Abrams tanks would shred the Russian tanks to ribbons from range. When that was done, Bravo Company's infantry would roll in under cover of smoke and take out the dazed survivors of a blistering artillery barrage that would blanket the dug-in positions for ten straight minutes. Textbook.

Now all bets were off. The quote 'ideal' unquote counterattack location was anything but.

"Do we have any planes operating in the area? Maybe precision-guided munitions could take out those tanks and soften up the infantry…" Mackinsky's voice trailed off.

Clifton glanced down at his clipboard and leafed through a few pages.

"Uh, sir. All our aircraft are either already committed or tasked with operations further east right now. The Soviets managed to take out a few of our airbases with bombing runs and Spetsnaz attacks. We're still recovering from that."

Mackinsky drummed his knuckles on the wooden desktop. He was out of answers. "What do you propose?"

"The only way to avoid killing all those people in Fulda," said Clifton, "is to leave it alone."

Mackinsky pulled the map over and swept the magnifying glass from the table. His eyes were getting old and the hours spent squinting at these things were not helping matters. Several small towns no more substantial than an ink blot sat five kilometers from the northernmost point of Fulda. One of them had a bridge. It was just a five-millimeter black dash on the paper.

"This town here. Lüdermünd. It's got a bridge over the Fulda, right?"

Clifton leaned over the map and ran a finger along the highway that ran north from Fulda until the tip of his nail met the "münd" part of "Lüdermünd." A few minutes later, an aide was summoned, and a topographical map was delivered that zoomed in on the key features of the area. It turned out that no less than three of the villages to the north of Fulda had bridges that spanned the river.

Kämmerzell, Lüdermünd, and Hemmen were tiny farming communities that had sat on the edge of the Fulda River for centuries, using its water to irrigate the plentiful wheat and barley crops that grew tall in the valleys of Hessen.

A glimmer of hope flickered in Mackinsky's mind. Maybe the operation could be salvaged after all - with slight modifications. The US V Corps commander would get his bridges back. Mackinsky would get his counterattack. Best of all, the West German civilians in Fulda wouldn't have to get pummeled by an artillery barrage that would reduce them all to a fine paste.

"What if we take these towns instead?" he asked. "Leave Fulda alone and just focus on these smaller objectives. I know it's not as sexy but -"

"Okay, let's see."

Clifton rubbed his eyes and leafed through the worn pages of his notepad. He gazed at the map and punched in numbers on a calculator. Mackinsky sat in silence and tried hard not to give off the vibe that he was impressed. If this were medieval Europe, the slight man with the thick spectacles in front of him would no doubt be Merlin. And Mackinsky himself would be some poor schmuck trying to rally his beleaguered troops at the gates of Jerusalem.

When Clifton was done, he slipped the pen back into his pocket and slapped the cover of the book.

"We have eyes on the ground there. Reports have indicated a re-inforced motorized rifle company near the west bank and a couple of infantry platoons scattered through the towns. Several tanks have been spotted further to the east. We can shift some of our scouts up there to get a better look."

Mackinsky nodded. "Do it."

He looked down at the map and examined the landscape near the towns. Fox Troop could clear out the defenses on the west bank. Bravo Company would make a quick thrust through Hemmen and over the river before turning south to take Lüdermünd. That would deny the Soviets two bridges. Delta's tanks would move east and take out the Soviet tanks east of the town. The critical problem was the infantry. Mackinsky didn't have enough men or enough time to secure both towns. He had just enough for one.

For the plan to work, the defenses in and around Hemmen would need to be pummeled. Again, it all came down to a question of artillery.

"Are there…any civilians in Hemmen?" he said. His voice was wounded and filled with regret for even asking the question.

Clifton dug out a single photograph and laid it out in front of Mackinsky.

In the center of the frame sat a BMP on a street corner. Behind it, the bungalows were lined up along the road in a neat little row. The nearest home had a white picket fence. Beyond that, in one of the windows, was the unmistakable silhouette of two figures. One was slim and feminine with long hair. The other was much smaller - a child. The next frame showed the same scene, but this time the curtains were drawn.

His insides twisted. Suddenly all the talk about "acceptable civilian casualties" during REFORGER exercises no longer seemed entirely theoretical. Still, what could be done? The Soviets were playing games with NATO's conscience, setting up shop in towns full of civilians and daring NATO to come for them. The scheme was diabolical. Thousands in Fulda would be spared at the expense of fewer innocent lives up in Hemmen. Mackinsky was forced to play god now, and he didn't like it one bit. He ought to just kick the whole operation back to General Basevi and let him choose another commander.

He stared at the mother and child frozen in the photo and spoke to himself.

"I always believed that at the end of my life, I'd get the chance to plunge my hand down into the bucket of well-intentioned swill that my existence created and maybe pluck out one or two things I'd done. Something that I could hold up to my maker and say, 'Here. Look. My life had value. It had worth.' Now though…"

Clifton took a step back.

"Sir, do you want to cancel the whole thing?"

Mackinsky set the photo down gently and laced his fingers together. Redemption was out of reach. Someone had to die. Making the decision to kill civilians was monstrous. Passing that responsibility on to someone else was unforgivable.

"Cliff, I want you to brief the commanders on the ground and update them on the new objectives. I'll let Basevi know this thing is a green light."

The major grabbed all the photographs and maps on the table and slid them into a manila envelope.

Mackinsky stood up and cleared his throat. "One more thing before you go, major. Burn all those photos. This conversation never happened."

"Yes, sir."

HIGH SCORE

Sergeant Harland sat in the gunner's seat of an Abrams tank wrapped in a beautiful bubble of technology.

Through the foam headphones over his ears, Motley Crue shouted at the devil at full blast on his Sony Walkman. The soft glow of the portable Coleco perched on his lap lit the dark interior of the tank. With a twitch of his index finger, his little space ship wound through the maze of enemies and brick walls on the tiny screen. This version of Zaxxon wasn't as good as playing in the arcade, but it helped beat back the crushing boredom of waiting around for things to happen - a time-honored feature of military service even during a major war.

Just before he reached his three millionth point, daylight flooded down into the turret. Harland's spaceship disappeared in the glare.

"Hey!" he heard himself shout. "Close that damn hatch."

Travers poked his head down inside and jabbed a finger in Harland's direction. The el-tee was saying something, but Mick Mars was right in the middle of a screaming guitar solo. Harland fumbled with the Walkman, and the tape screeched to a halt. Too late. Whatever pejoratives were used as a preamble to address Harland were lost to the ages.

"-kinsky needs a driver. Get going."

Ignoring the chuckles from Rodriguez and Simonsen, Harland climbed up out of the turret. He knew it should have bothered him, but it didn't. There really was nothing for a gunner to do while the tank was waiting to be fueled up. And besides that, the interior reeked of unwashed bodies and MRE-induced flatulence.

The outside world was awash in the powerful mechanics of the turbine. The refueling process was taking ages since security was of the utmost importance. Instead of lining up for gas like a bunch of dummies, each tank had to come out from its dug-in position, take on a load of fuel and then drive on to a new dug-in position about five hundred meters down the road. Then the next tank would do the same. So an operation that would have usually taken around an hour in peacetime now took nearly all morning.

Harland's knees buckled a bit as he hit the ground and jogged for the cover of the trees. Under a tangle of leaves and branches sat the old rusting jeep, a relic of so many wars past. And here it was, in 1985, still in service to a superpower army. Harland swept away the last of the pine needles from the seat cushion and shifted into gear. The little vehicle grumbled as its engine came to life.

A two minute drive through the West German countryside was all it took to reach the Battalion HQ. Before he could even light a cigarette, Mackinsky walked out. Harland shot up to attention.

"At ease, son," commanded the colonel. He sat down in the vehicle as a helicopter chattered nearby. As if to announce the arrival of the man, a wave of artillery crashed down somewhere off to the northeast.

"Let's go to Fox."

The colonel said almost nothing along the way. On previous trips, the old man had spent the entire time regaling Harland with stories about fishing and hunting in Louisiana, the home state they both shared. Harland would listen politely and nod along at the right parts, but the truth was that his father had left the family early on and his mother had never cultivated the boy's interest in the outdoors. While Jean May Harland slaved away at two and occasionally three minimum wage jobs, the boy was parked alone in front of a TV or pile of comic books for hours at a time.

And while Sergeant Harland usually had no idea what the old man was talking about, it seemed rude to strip him of the illusion of some mutual interest. The gears clattered as he downshifted and the jeep bumbled up the hillside.

Harland stomped the brakes just short of a Bradley that sat near the roadside. Its innards had been gutted and the M240 machine gun removed. One of the mechanics wandered out from the back of the vehicle as Mackinsky got out and strode off in search of Fox Troop's commander.

Harland hauled out the worn Stephen King paperback from his pocket and leafed through the dog-eared pages until he found where he had left off. He'd read this one so many times, he almost didn't need the book anymore, but something was comforting about it. This one was about a guy who could see hidden things about people just by touching them. The idea intrigued Harland. If he had such a power, would he see his Rodriguez and Simonsen going home at the end of the war? Maybe he would see their final moments before the world went up in flames and everything around them burned.

The horrific visions that swirled in his head were banished by the hammer of knuckles on the jeep's hood. In front of the vehicle stood the mechanic, a lanky E-2 who looked like he was about ready to drop.

"You got a minute?" he asked.

Harland recognized the drawl as backcountry West Virginia. It was the kind of voice that would cheerfully tell a stranded motorist that the price for a blown gasket was three times more than the quote. He creased the corner of the page and set down the novel.

"What can I do for you?"

The mechanic sniffed and pointed to the broken Bradley.

"Gotta salvage these parts. Need someone to help hammer the tread out."

He spat on the ground and eyed Harland's shoulder patch insignia. A few seconds later, he added in the requisite "sar'nt."

Harland shot a glance over to the trees where Mackinsky had disappeared. Knowing the old man, he might take anywhere from five minutes to three hours.

He could have blown off the mechanic, but the book would wait, as it always did. The specialist pointed over to a ten-pound sledgehammer, and Harland nearly groaned. Well, it seemed too late to back out now. The two men wandered over to the shell of the vehicle. The rear ramp had a pair of fist-sized holes punched through it. The interior of the vehicle was a dark stain - as if someone had thrown an open can of paint inside. Harland halted in his tracks. Just seeing something like this seemed like bad luck.

"Whatsa matter, sar'ent? You ain't seen no blowed up vee-hick-als 'afore?"

The mechanic stared back at him with the slightest of grins and Harland wasn't sure if the man was mocking him or asking him a sincere question. There was something evil about this whole situation. The hairs stood up on the end of his neck. He felt like he had fallen into the depths of one of his Stephen King novels. He decided to assert control.

"Private, I'm a tank gunner. I don't just look at torn up vehicles. I make 'em that way."

The mechanic eyeballed him long enough for Harland to sense his words being weighed and measured. Finally, he shrugged and dipped a hand in the toolbox on the ground. Harland's unease about the grease monkey only grew. It was almost like this guy knew some terrible secret.

Harland lugged the sledgehammer to his shoulder and slammed it down against the edge of the tread. The thing didn't even budge.

"You gotta hit it harder'n that, sar'ent."

Harland sniffed away the shot to his pride.

"Just getting warmed up. You been with the 2nd ACR the whole time?"

A line of snuff shot down into the dirt.

"The whole time."

The mechanic straightened his back and lifted his chin. A pair of half-lidded eyes looked down on Harland, daring him to ask another question.

The sledgehammer swung down again. CLANG! This time the track inched off the return roller.

"What happened to this one?" Something deep down in Harland felt like he was opening a door that should have remained shut.

"This one? Just like the others in Fox. Shot to pieces from the rear." The mechanic threw a lazy finger in the direction of the ramp. "This one got hit real bad. Probably thirty mike mike at close range from a BMP-2. Went clean through. Killed nearly ev'rbuddy in it. Had to use the pressure washer on the inside. You shoulda seen it when it rolled in, sar'ent. Arms and legs ever-where."

Harland squeezed out a breath and brought the hammer down again. The tread dangled halfway off now. Another hit or two should do it.

"You get a lot of these?"

The mechanic shrugged. "The whole maintenance unit's workin' over yonder. We pick through whatever comes back and fix up what we can. Everything here is just pieces of other vehicles now. Sometimes we get replacement parts come in. Lotsa stuff we don't need or can't use."

"That sucks," said Harland. Another heave of the hammer and the tread slipped off its mooring. The sweat dripped along his face. He dropped the tool in the dirt.

The mechanic poked through the coiled treads that sat on the ground. Without looking up, he spoke words that sunk deep into Harland's brain.

"Nah. What sucks is bein' one of you guys. The things I seen today I cain't never unsee. My daddy used to skin deer while I watched. I never felt bad for the deer. But you guys," he said. "I feel sorry for you."

Harland couldn't contain himself any longer. "How are the Abrams doing out there?"

"They hold their own, I reckon. Some of 'em ain't come back. Most of their crews do though," the mechanic said.

The trees rustled and Mackinsky walked towards the jeep. The old man's expression was as hard as shale as he climbed into the jeep. The leader of Fox Company, Lieutenant Harris stumbled through next. Not a light flickered in the man's eyes. Harland got into the driver's seat and wondered not for the first what he had gotten himself into.

IRON HORSE

1 km north of Bimbach

Captain Tony Costa sat under the shade of a tree and mulled over the thick stack of papers that Colonel Mackinsky, the task force commander had just handed him. Since the very first shots had been fired, Fox's men had run their own little war against the 8th Guards Tank Army. They had set up careful ambushes and hit out at the Soviets at every single opportunity as they advanced west. 2/11 had kicked some serious butt and left behind a long string of destroyed enemy tanks and fighting vehicles all the way back to the inner German border.

But the problem, as it always had been, was that there was just never enough. Retreat after retreat had followed from Phase Line Alpha all the way to Phase Line Delta. Each step of the way, the armored cavalry troop would punch the advance elements in the nose only to watch as the follow-up echelons took their place and advanced further west. There seemed to be no end to the suffering and death the enemy was willing to accept to move up a kilometer here or there.

Though he'd been trained amply for it, he was shocked by the war's pace and rate of consumption. Like a giant maw, the conflict demanded vast amounts of everything and was never satisfied.

Fox had fed its penchant for blood and destruction at the cost of a dozen good men and a platoon of tanks. The replacements had trickled in all morning, and they were getting quick briefs from the other men about the ins and outs of facing down the Russians. As he had expected, the veterans provided the newcomers with a chilly reception, but they were doing as ordered and that's all that really mattered.

Costa leafed through the orders and noted the changes that Mackinsky had personally warned him about. The previous plan to attack Fulda had been shelved in favor of something less ambitious. Instead of storming into the town and reclaiming Downs Barracks for the Blackhorse Regiment, his troop would be leading an attack to capture the bridges to the north. Costa didn't ask why - he didn't need to. His scouts had been working out there with jeeps and Kiowa helicopters to locate the enemy and gather as much information about the area as they could. The reports had trickled back to him about the civilians in Fulda, and he guessed that Mackinsky didn't have the stomach to ruin their day by flattening their homes with a rain of 155-millimeter shells.

The change in plans wasn't necessarily a bad thing. Costa could see the concrete benefits of such a move. Any counterattack would carry with it the same desirable result. The Russians would have to watch their flanks and deploy more security elements alongside their main axis of advance. That would mean reducing the numbers of enemy tanks that would be sent to the front. The concept of a counterattack was filed away in Costa's head as a good enough reason to risk his men and tanks to achieve.

If they got really lucky and captured the bridges, that would worsen the narrow bottleneck of traffic that the Soviets were struggling to widen. It was true that the northern bridges were minor ones and the Soviets didn't really need them to keep the attack going. But their loss would surely be felt while the long line of vehicles and men piled up near the Fulda River. When NATO air came back online, the enemy armor would be sitting ducks for the A-10s and Cobras. It would be a slaughter.

The best part, though, was that Costa would have his revenge. He had lost some good men this morning - guys whom he counted as friends. The Russians would need to pay for that, and this was his golden chance. He rubbed his hands together and leafed through Mackinsky's typed orders.

The scheme of maneuver was simple, and the colonel had been clear enough with his intent. Two motorized rifle companies were in the area of Lüdermünd. One was on the west side of the Fulda River with infantry and tanks parked up on the reverse slope of the hills near Hemmen. The other sat on the east side of the river with about two platoons worth of infantry in Lüdermünd and the rest of the company further east of the town. Mackinsky wanted to clear the Soviets away from both sides of the river. Once that was done, they'd set up a security position that would allow a stream of tanks and men from the rest of the 8th Infantry Division to create a wedge-shaped dent in the Soviet advance.

Fox Troop was to hammer the enemy's defensive approaches west of Hemmen at Objective Knight. Once that was cleared, the 8th Infantry Division would enter the picture. The town itself would be hit with a hail of artillery and Bravo would rush over the nearby bridge and turn south to capture Lüdermünd, dubbed Objective Rook. While the town was being seized, two platoons of tanks from Delta would advance, attacking the enemy positions to the east of town at Objective Queen. A tank platoon from Delta would work with a platoon of Fox's Bradleys to scoot behind the dug-in enemy position to create a blocking force at Objective King. When the Russians tried to pull back east, they would find themselves trapped between two companies. The plan was to obliterate the Russian presence around the town altogether. The key to success was lightning speed. If Soviet reinforcements arrived at any point, the Americans would have to stop whatever they were doing and orient to the new threat.

It went without saying that the entire operation was being kept under tight wraps. For any of it to work, the Russians had to be taken by complete surprise. To that effect, Mackinsky had taken great care to disguise what was really happening here in the woods to the northwest of Fulda. Several two-man counter-reconnaissance teams had been dispatched since Costa's arrival in the area.

Costa had set up no less than three concentric rings of ambushes, booby traps, automatic claymores, and mines around his troop. Any curious 'razvedka' teams that got too close would find themselves caught in a deadly quagmire of hot death.

To add to the illusion, Costa had sent a pair of Bradleys and an Abrams to run laps around the outskirts of the valley to the west to draw the attention of the enemy scouts. He had also dispatched three two-man radio teams into the villages a few kilometers away. The guys had spent all morning talking to each other on an unencrypted channel, sending false messages back and forth. Someone had the bright idea of setting up a fake TOC in the parking lot of a Wendy's way over in Grossenlüder. The end result was to make it look and sound like the US Army was withdrawing troops further west to consolidate their strength at the next phase line. It wouldn't be too much of a stretch to believe since it was precisely what they had been doing since the war had begun.

The opening for the attack had been conceived as part of a deception as well. Although it was hard to disguise the sound of a company of armored vehicles, the geography of Fulda had a habit of warping acoustics in a way that made it hard to pinpoint from where the noise emanated. The Soviets had discovered this early on and had used it to their advantage several times. Now they would find that the game went both ways. The troop's maintenance vehicles would accompany Fox's tanks to the limits of the line of departure and veer off to the south, making it sound like the second prong of an attack was on the way. The 2/11 artillery squadron would lay down a curtain of smoke far to the south of the main approach, thereby adding to the illusion.

While Costa's company of tanks and men kept out of sight by driving through the depressions among the hills, the Russian commander would see the smoke and hear the maintenance vehicles. Hopefully, he would orient his defenses to meet a non-existent enemy coming from the southwest. When the smoke dissipated to reveal only the light of day, Costa's lead tanks would already be pulverizing the Soviets at Objective Knight, and Bravo would be over the bridge at Hemmen and driving hell for leather toward Rook.

It was a good plan, and he couldn't help smile at the look on the Russians' faces when they would pop up over the last hill and open up without hesitation.

Costa thumbed past the pages of written orders and ran down the list of radio callsigns, known as a "cheat sheet." The battalion commander had taken "Wildman" for himself. Fox was designated "Firefox" while Delta was "Dragon" and Bravo took "Bearclaw." Other callsigns were assigned to various assets such as the artillery officer and mortar section. The companies were all communicating together on the same battalion net, which would make Mackinsky's job easier to coordinate them all. That sounded good, but in Costa's experience, it created a potential hazard. When guys got excited, they started talking over each other, and things got confusing very quickly. He had tried to bring it up with Mackinsky, but the man wouldn't have it.

"Simplicity is key," he had insisted.

The biggest worry was the infantry. Only three platoons of M113s were available to carry the infantry to Objective Rook. Mackinsky had tried to cover all the bases by ordering each infantry platoon to have a pair of men with a Stinger missile launcher assigned to air defense. One APC from each platoon would carry four combat engineers to help remove obstacles in the town of Lüdermünd and then wire the bridges to blow in case things went south and the Soviets came charging back hard to reclaim them. With limited space available in the APCs, that meant one regular infantry squad from each platoon had to be sacrificed to fit the engineers and the AD teams. In effect, only two combat infantry platoons would be charging into Lüdermünd. So much for simplicity.

The rest of the pages were filled with maps of the area, photocopies of sketches from the scouts, weather reports, and topographical information. Mackinsky had been meticulous with his preparations. In a matter of a few short hours, Costa's scouts would direct the task force to their positions and act as traffic guides to get them all safely to the line of departure. All that was left for Costa to do was to devise a cohesive plan for his platoons and sections to follow, brief each platoon leader, and carry out a pre-combat inspection. He had learned early on that it was impossible to do all of these things, but he would try anyway.

He reached over and grabbed a fistful of soft earth, slapping it between his palms until he had a ball of clay. This would be the hillside of Objective Knight where a motorized rifle regiment would be wiped from the face of the planet. Next, he clipped a branch from a nearby tree and broke off a twig. He laid it to the right of Knight. This was the bridge over the Fulda that lead to Hemmen. A few stones represented the town that would be flattened by artillery early on. An old bootlace represented the little road that went south towards Lüdermünd. The squads would dismount somewhere near the southern tip and kill off the Russians inside the town, which was a dented Coca Cola bottle cap that he found under the soft soil. Two clumps of earth represented the hills to the east of the city where Objective King and Queen sat.

He looked down upon his work and smiled. It wasn't great, but it was good enough, and that would have to do. His muscles ached as he got up and wandered over to where his platoon leaders were wolfing down MRE lunches heated up by vehicle engines.

"Gentlemen," he announced. "We're having a working lunch. Come with me. Let's go over the plan for today."

KNIGHT

Costa rode in the cupola of his M1 tank and savored the moment as his tank reached the line of departure. This was the last simple moment of peace before the storm broke out. Far to the south, the smoke rounds were billowing up from the narrow pass that marked the gap between two huge hills that were nestled against the Fulda River. In front of him were his Bradleys and the other tanks of the company, staying low among the hilly approach to the northeast. The scouts stood out in the clear, waving the vehicles this way and that, showing them the way to the enemy. It wasn't Costa's first time in combat, but it was the first time he was in an attack. It felt so much better than defense.

Instead of worrying about where the enemy would come from and what assets he would deploy against him, it was his turn to seize the initiative and turn it all around on them. One of the traffic directors gave him a salute as he passed and Costa shot it back. The afternoon sunlight shone down into the little valleys and blanketed everything around him in a soft golden hue. He was Hannibal at Cannae. Alexander at Issus. Lee at Chancellorsville.

What a great day to be alive and in combat.

When the tanks broke through the hills to the north, there was no hesitation. Firing while on the move, the first volley of Abrams fire sliced deep into the ranks of the defending T-62s. Within the first thirty seconds, a Soviet tank platoon parked in the open field was wiped out.

The entire Abrams platoon turned in unison and formed an echelon right while it wheeled counter-clockwise around the outskirts of the town. The Bradleys parked on the hillsides to the south unleashed their TOW missiles at a pair of infantry carriers on the other side of the river. No doubt, the Soviet commander had recalled them south, expecting the Americans to rush out of the smoke barrage and head straight over the bridge near Lüdermünd.

As his platoon of M1s plowed through the fields, a fountain of dirt jumped up over his tank and coated the turret with dark soil. Costa turned his attention to the town of Hemmen and scanned for the source of the fire. A platoon of tanks was pulling back from the fields and into the town itself. The first wrinkle in the plan was now apparent. The Soviet commander was pulling back all his vehicles east across the river. The ruse with the smoke barrage had perhaps been too effective. Those T-62s needed to die now.

Costa ordered his M1 to halt while the other three vehicles in the platoon resumed their wheel. His gunner caught a peek of a tank skirting among the houses of Hemmen and fired. The T-62 brewed up, taking out chunks of a nearby duplex. The formerly neat lawn upon which the dead tank now sat was ablaze. Alpha One Two's tank reported a kill at nearly the same time, and Costa wasn't entirely sure if he was claiming the T-62 his gunner had just pasted or whether a second tank in the town was dead. While he was sorting it out with the platoon sergeant, Mackinsky came over the radio and demanded an update. Something streaked over Costa's head and struck one of Bravo's APCs a hundred yards behind him. The little vehicle was ripped open.

Fox tried to sort out what was happening. Why were Bravo's carriers so close behind him? They should have waited until Fox announced the all clear. Even then, the artillery barrage was supposed to come next. Before he could contact Mackinsky, one of his Abrams to the north reported a track hit. They were stuck in the middle of the field, taking fire from a Sagger team in the town. Meanwhile, Bravo's captain came over the battalion net instead of the company net to try and haul back his M113s.

Which crisis did he deal with first? He forced back the panic and spoke with the task force commander.

FIREFOX MAIN TO WILDMAN. HOSTILE TANKS ARE AT OBJECTIVE ROOK AND FIRING BACK ON US. THE AREA AROUND KNIGHT IS TOO DANGEROUS. BEARCLAW IS TOO CLOSE TO THE OBJECTIVE AND TAKING HEAVY FIRE. ADVISE YOU PULL BACK BEARCLAW UNTIL WE TAKE CARE OF IT. OVER.

As he was waiting for a response, an M113 rolled straight past his tank and headed straight for the town. Costa waved his arms and screamed at the vehicle commander but failed to gain his attention. Two more APCs followed. Costa resisted the urge to get on the battalion net and talk back the APCs. Instead, he focused his attention on his own men. The Bradleys in 2nd Platoon were still sitting on the hillside but no longer finding targets on the far side of the river. If the M113s were headed towards the town, the best thing that Fox Troop could do was to offer cover fire for the unexpected advance.

FIREFOX 6 TO FIREFOX RED 6. SCAN FOR ANY TARGETS IN THE TOWN AND PROVIDE SUPPRESSIVE COVER FIRE FOR BEARCLAW, OVER.

Another Sagger leaped out from the town and missed the lead M113 by a dozen yards. The 25mm automatic cannons from Costa's Bradleys opened up, peppering the town with thousands of rounds. Big puffs of dust bounced up from the buildings as the fire swept in. Mackinsky's voice poured in on the radio, addressing the artillery officer with colorful language. Apparently, the task force commander had decided that if he was unable to rein in Bravo, he would order in the fire mission early on.

While Bravo was halfway to Objective Knight, the artillery arrived. The rounds came in all at once. A giant curtain of fire screeched down over Hemmen and splashed down like a huge wave. Hot air rushed past Costa's face. Eruptions of detritus and debris leaped upwards in the grey billowing cloud. Through the gunner's thermals, he saw not a single building standing in the Hemmen. The place had not only been destroyed - it had been crushed into powdered dust.

Mackinsky shouted over the radio like a man on fire.

WILDMAN TO BEARCLAW. ADVANCE ON ROOK! GO NOW! GO!

ROOK

Captain Harris hacked and wheezed as his command APC lumbered through the debris of the town formerly known as Hemmen. Its twenty-odd homes and handful of little shops were just a memory now. After the crushing wave of artillery had blasted the town, he had expected to find the gruesome sight of bodies waiting for him. But there was nothing left of whoever had been here, and somehow that was even more disturbing. But what really bothered the leader of Bravo Company was that he was utterly lost amid the thick choking dust.

By now, he should have crossed over the bridge that spanned the Fulda River and been halfway to Objective Rook. Instead, his M113 had been rolling over chest-high rubble for three minutes.

Mackinsky's voice intruded over the radio set yet again.

WILDMAN TO BEARCLAW. HURRY UP AND GET OVER THE BRIDGE. FRIENDLY SMOKE MISSION ABOUT TO ARRIVE TO THE EAST OF YOUR POSITION, OVER.

Asking Mackinsky for help was out of the question. A court-martial would be the least of his worries when the old man got his hands on him. Instead, Harris slid back down into the APC and shouted at the driver.

"You see the bridge yet?"

"I can't see anything through all this crap!"

"Well…keep driving!"

Delta's tanks would have undoubtedly found the bridge without a problem since the thermal sights would see right through all the crud floating through the air. If they could latch on to one of the stragglers, maybe Harris had a chance of finding the way.

"Hey, private! You see a tank out there, you follow it. Hear me?"

"Yes, sir," he mumbled.

The kid had given up. If they were going to get out of here, Harris would need to do it. With a curse, he threw on his gas mask then popped up out of the hatch. Though it was stifling and his field of vision was limited, he could at least breathe without having to ingest a lungful of debris. His surroundings came slowly into focus.

The M113 bounded over another hill composed of the smashed remains of a two-story house. A flattened Volkswagen sat under a pile of wood and brick. There was something familiar about it. He ducked down into the APC and smacked the kid on the helmet.

"Hey! Idiot! We're driving in circles. Stop and orient yourself."

While Mackinsky pleaded over the radio for Bravo to get going, Harris popped out of the hatch once again and whipped off the gas mask. The heavy reeking air drifted away on a gentle breeze. The smoke thinned just enough to reveal the fuzzy outline of trees that lined the opposite bank of the river. Harris tapped the edge of his boot on the driver's shoulder, and the APC climbed over another jumble of smashed brick and churned soil. Directly to his right lay the bridge. As if by some miracle, its two lanes were still intact. Two platoons' worth of M113s were already across and driving towards Rook. Smoke wafted up to the skies a hundred meters east of their position.

Harris' vehicle jolted forward across the bridge as the driver stomped on the pedal and cackled. After a minute of pedal-to-the-metal driving, the M-113 arrived at the rear of the column of tanks and APCs. A quick radio call to Mackinsky assured him that Bravo was on the way to Rook at full speed. A platoon of Delta's tanks shot forward into the lead while the other eight tanks swerved east and disappeared into the wall of smoke. As Harris approached the town, the plan of attack congealed in his head once again.

Recon reports showed the north and south routes into Lüder-münd were mined, and a few concrete barriers had been set up on the main approaches to impede the progress of armor vehicles. To the east of the town lay a handful of earthen trenches manned by two squads of infantry. The original plan had been to mount a three-pronged attack on Rook with friendly armor supporting the main effort to the east. Considering the losses that Bravo had taken from missile and tank fire near Knight, that seemed impossible. The numbers just weren't there anymore. Harris shook his head at the map in his hands and went with his instincts. A small force would be sent to tie the Soviets down on the north side of the town while everyone else hooked east and attacked. It was going to be a tough fight.

He switched over to the company network and spoke up.

BEARCLAW MAIN TO ALL BEARCLAW ELEMENTS. DISMOUNT YOUR SQUADS THREE HUNDRED METERS EAST OF ROOK. BEARCLAW RED WILL PROVIDE COVER FIRE. BEARCLAW BLUE WILL MOVE TOGETHER WITH THE TANKS.

A sour taste filled his mouth. He was trained to be flexible and adapt to situations, but this sudden shift opened up new possibil-ities for things to go horribly wrong. To make it work, he'd have to lead from the front and show what he wanted to be done and where.

"Get on the road!" he shouted to his driver.

"But you said there's mines-."

"Just get on the road! Get ahead of everyone. I want you to swing around to the southeast after about two hundred meters. Do it!"

The APC thumped over the lip of the pavement and accelerated past the trailing APCs of Bravo Company. Harris scanned the road's surface for any sign of mines, but there was debris all over from the artillery strike on Hemmen. Standing in the cupola of a vehicle traveling at 60 kilometers an hour, there was no way he could pick out a piece of furniture from an anti-tank mine. He cringed as the APC rolled straight over a pile of junk that could have very well concealed an explosive device.

It felt like playing Russian roulette with an 11-ton vehicle.

When he reached the front of the column, he ordered the APCs to fan out into a wedge formation a hundred meters behind the Abrams. Three hundred meters to the north of the town, Harris ordered a pair of Abrams to halt. A rocket slammed into the ground fifty meters in front of the group. One of the tanks belted out a high explosive round in response.

Using hand signals, Harris got the attention of 1st Platoon's commander and told him to leave a squad behind. One of the M113s pulled up behind the tanks and disgorged the men into a gully that ran perpendicular to the road. No sooner had the dismounted squad set up a pair of M60s when rifle fire broke out from the nearest buildings about three hundred meters away. The tanks fired again, carving a couple of bus-sized holes into the squat building.

Harris pointed his driver to the southeast, and the remaining vehicles left the road with two of Delta's tanks in the lead. The tracks of the APCs cut a pair of lines through the knee-high grass on the outskirts of the town. Small arms fire poured out at them, forcing Harris to duck back inside the M113. A quick check of the map gave him a rough idea of his position. A few hundred yards from here sat clumps of trees and brush amid several large grassy mounds. From there, he would have just enough cover to launch an assault on the trenches. With any luck, the group he had left behind to the north of the town would keep the Russians pinned down and distracted. The last thing he needed right now was to get into a protracted firefight against a reinforced enemy.

The APCs formed a line abreast with the Abrams on the right side in a bid to protect the carriers from anti-tank fire from the town. Sure enough, a pair of rocket-propelled grenades swooped down from the top of a grain silo. One of them crunched into the soil while the other bounced off the hull side of an M1. The tank did not even pause in its progress. Its turret swung ninety degrees, and the main gun hurled a high explosive round back at the silo. The twisted metal frame teetered and collapsed to the ground and lay there like a child's broken toy.

Through the vision blocks, Harris caught a glimpse of the enemy defenses. From the trench line, a stream of tracers skimmed just above the ground towards the APCs. Metal shards bounced against the APCs before his group descended along a steep depression. It was here that he called for a halt. The ramps slammed down, and the men ran out of the APCs. Harris found Jim Neeson, his company sergeant, busy setting up the flank security teams while the rest of the men spread out as they had rehearsed. The infantry were at their most vulnerable while mounting and dismounting. All it would take was a mortar team to zero in on their position and ruin everyone's day.

Neeson acknowledged Harris' approach with a nod.

"You see that trench about two hundred meters from here? I want that dead space covered by mortars and grenade launchers," said Harris. "Oh yeah. Let the air defense teams and engineers know that they're back to being grunts." Harris cast an eye up to the deep blue sky and wondered what would happen if a Hind came along to ruin his day. It wasn't out of the question that the Soviets would call in air support, but that seemed a possibility rather than an actuality. On the other hand, the Soviet infantry firing machine guns at them from two hundred meters away seemed pretty real.

Neeson got to work on the radio, checking grid coordinates and calling in fire from Fox Troop's M106 mortar carrier.

The clatter of the .50 caliber weapons fire from the M113s was like a jackhammer against Harris' head. But there wasn't much to be done about it. He knew he had to learn to think despite all the distractions and noise of combat. His brain was still catching up to his surroundings by the time he took serious measure of how the hasty assault into the town was going to work.

After what seemed like forever, he located his 1st and 2nd Platoon leaders and brought them together with Neeson for a quick field briefing.

"We've got a trench line to our front about two hundred meters. I want it taken out. When the mortars stop, I want two elements to provide support fire with machine guns and grenade launchers. When I give the signal, the tanks move forward, and the assault team goes around the right flank and hits it hard."

A few minutes later, the radio acknowledgments came from each platoon commander. Grenades and mortar fire splashed down to the front for two solid minutes. Harris gave the "Go" signal, and the tanks rolled forward on cue. As they met the lip of the trench, a firefight broke out on the right-hand side and the sound of men screaming and dying pierced through the hellish soundscape of death and machinery. The Abrams commanders tilted their .50 caliber machine guns down into the trench and opened fire to their front. It was all over in less than a minute.

Harris didn't get the chance to be impressed. Something sharp slapped against one of the tanks near the trench line. A quick radio call from the tank commander confirmed his worst fears. His Abrams had taken an RPG hit to the hull bottom. Spalling had seriously injured the driver, but the rest of the crew was untouched. So now he would be going into the east of Lüdermünd with one tank for support. He was about to call over the tanks from the north side of the town but dismissed the idea. It would take too long, and he couldn't afford to have the Russians figure out that his left flank was wide open to a counterattack. There was no time left.

Every soldier armed with a grenade launcher fired a smoke round along the path of Bravo's planned approach. When the outskirts of the town were enveloped in a misty haze of gray, it was time to go. With the APCs firing over their heads, Harris and his men crouched and ran forward toward the town. Harris followed a squad through a massive hole cut into an old wooden house. Judging from the smashed television in the corner and the overturned couches, he was in a huge living room. Something flashed by on his right, and he fired a three-round burst that punched into a refrigerator door in the next room. From less than six meters away, a head popped up over a countertop, and two of Harris' men loosened a hail of rounds at the figure.

After a heavy moment of silence, Harris got up and walked into the kitchen with his M16 at the ready. A heavyset bearded man lay still on the hardwood floor in a pool of his own blood. He closed his eyes and heaved a sigh.

"Civilian," he declared. "We got a dead civilian here."

The men glanced around at each other then looked back at him expectantly. What could he do? Halt the advance and report to Mackinsky? His men were now scattered throughout the town and his command APC was a hundred meters away across an open field. He might as well have tried to stop the wind from blowing. The only thing left was to warn the men. He grabbed his radioman and keyed the handset.

BEARCLAW TO ALL BEARCLAW ELEMENTS. WATCH YOUR FIRE. WE HAVE POSSIBLE CIVILIANS IN THE AREA. I REPEAT WATCH YOUR FIRE, OVER.

Harris gathered the squad around him and spoke up.

"Alright, listen. We have a civilian casualty here. That's on the Russians. Not you. I want you all to continue doing your jobs as you're trained. New rules of engagement from now on. First, confirm your targets before you fire. Second, no throwing grenades blind. Other than that, we do what we came here to do. Got it?"

The men nodded. Harris stood up. "Alright then. Let's take this damn town!"

QUEEN

Delta's tanks hooked around the base of the peanut-shaped hill that sat half a kilometer east of Lüdermünd. Harland caught sight of the reverse side of the slope where a group of T-55s and BMPs sat. They were easy to make out in thermal mode, with their vehicle bodies bathed in the white glow of his screen. Travers shouted out the first target, a motionless tank less than a hundred and fifty meters from their position. Harland zoomed in on the T-55 at three times magnification and settled the targeting pip on the hull side, right where the fuel tank and ammunition sat. The M1 was still moving as he lased the target, but the gun was stabilized, and Harland felt none of the bumps or dips in the ground that his tank rode over.

Rodriguez shoved a SABOT round into the breech and screamed.

"Up!"

Harland depressed the trigger. A few feet away from in front of his face, the main gun boomed, slamming a new surge of adrenaline through his body and rattling his teeth. Almost instantly, the T-55 dissolved in a crisp white fireball.

"Hit!" he reported. "That smoked 'em!"

Three more shots rang out from the other tanks in 1st Platoon. The rest of the enemy T-55s on the slope were transformed into flaming piles of junk.

Travers got busy on the radio, leaving Harland to call his own targets. This was the best thing ever. It was just like being back home in the arcade, playing that one game where you looked through a periscope and shot other tanks to pieces. What was that one called? Oh yeah - Battlezone!

His dad had told him that fighting in Vietnam had been a living nightmare. But Harland didn't agree with that at all. Combat was rad. Especially when you could just look at your screen and press a few buttons and BLAMMO! The enemy was zapped.

With all four T-55s shot to pieces, he shifted his aim to the BMPs, which were now driving around in all directions. It was as if 1st Platoon had kicked over a hornet's nest. When Harland fired again, the tank round flung a Soviet infantry fighting vehicle several meters from the point of impact. It rolled six or seven times and stopped on its side. The thought that there were people inside the vehicles didn't really occur to him. He was having way too much fun.

Rodriguez demanded to know what was happening. Harland gave him the rundown as he lined up another target in his sights. One of the BMPs reversed down the hill and veered off to the north in a bid to escape the close range slaughter. 2nd Platoon rounded the hillside, and the little vehicle found itself caught between hammer and anvil. Two of the Abrams fired at almost the same time. Both rounds struck the hapless BMP, which was turned into an inferno of mangled steel. Travers spoke over the intercom, directing Simonsen further east towards Objective Queen. Harland scanned for any targets that might be sitting hull down on the hillside, but he couldn't find anything.

"Let's catch the next group with their pants down too," said the lieutenant. "Gunner. Watch out for 2nd Platoon. They're breaking around the other side of the hill."

Too easy. Harland chomped on his four pieces of Hubba Bubba and glued his eyeballs to the screen, switching from thermal to day mode and back again. Travers leaned forward to watch from his commander's sight. The first sign of trouble came ten seconds later. As they rounded a little fold in the hill, something hard smacked into the tank's armor side skirts. Harland cringed as two hard knocks shuddered against the turret. Before he could react, a fourth hit landed somewhere near the exposed rear drive sprocket. Typically, the skirt would cover that part of the tank, but it was standard procedure for Delta's crews to remove it. That way, the guard ring didn't get clogged with mud and throw a track. The tank ground to a sudden halt and all at once, the crew of The Terminator wished they hadn't taken off that portion of skirt armor.

The interior lights flickered. Harland was truly afraid for the very first time. The only way to douse the panic was to shoot back at whoever had dared to fire on them. He slew the turret in the direction of the hillside. Six or seven bad guys showed up on his screen as a white-hot blur.

Travers ducked down and let out a string of four letter words. "Loader! Didn't you hear me? Get on your weapon!"

Rodriguez pounced up like a coiled snake and threw his hatch open. Next came the knock-knock-knock of the fifty-cal.

Harland fired the 7.62 mm coax machine gun at the group of men less than a hundred meters away. The tracers from the tank's small arms fire zipped by on the thermals like pencil-thin blurs. The targets tumbled over and fell. He could tell when the commander's fifty-cal hit because the body just exploded. He had never seen that in any of his Atari or arcade games and something made him guffaw when he realized what was happening.

Travers slid back down into the turret and urged the rest of 1st Platoon to continue their advance around the side of the hill.

The engine whirred and screeched, and the tank wobbled forward a few meters before hitting another snag. It was as though the 60-ton vehicle had been yanked back on its leash like a bad dog. Harland watched through the sights as the rest of the platoon continued its sweep around the edge of the hill, eventually disappearing from view. The Terminator was alone now, and a sense of unease bubbled up inside the turret.

Rodriguez had ceased firing after loosening about a million rounds at the guys who had shot at them. Now, he sat beside Harland and rocked back and forth like a third grade kid who realized he had forgotten his homework for the dozenth time.

Travers had handed control of things to the platoon sergeant and now stood there uselessly in the cupola swearing at Simonsen as if will alone could repair the broken sprocket and realign the tracks. The shouting match resumed until Simonsen shouted, "Screw you, Lieutenant!" and refused to acknowledge any more of the tank commander's insane orders.

"Uh, sir…it doesn't look like we can go anywhere right now," said Harland. "Sergeant Haight probably has the situation control out there. Maybe it's time to call for a recovery vehicle and sit tight?"

The temperature fell about twenty degrees all of a sudden. Travers fiddled with the radio and gave a sitrep to Jenkins, the company commander. With a degree of snark in his voice, he added. "Oh yeah, my gunner would like to call for a recovery vehicle, sir."

Harland's shoulders sank to the floor. When the transmission mercifully ended, Travers informed the crew that Objective Queen had been taken, no thanks to their sorry butts. The lieutenant sat in a sulky silence while Harland kept facing forward, his focus stuck on the screen in front of him. He had never wanted to punch an officer so bad in his life.

Several minutes of tense silence followed as they waited for the armored recovery vehicle to come and remove the tank from the battlefield. After a long wait, Harland glimpsed the M88 in the gun sights. It ran down the long slope straight toward them, weaving around the crispy remains of enemy tanks and bodies that littered the hillside. Travers jumped down and approached it with his arms waving. The long crane-like appendage mounted on the Patton tank hull swung left and right as it maneuvered toward the M1. Simonsen stepped out from the driver's hatch and stretched.

"I'm gettin' out of here," announced Rodriguez.

Harland watched as the loader climbed out leaving him mercifully alone inside the vehicle. As he ran a hand along the Walkman that sat in his breast pocket, a shower of sparks flew up on the screen and the nails-on-chalkboard sound of screeching metal whipped through the air. Harland's eyes shot toward the gunner's screen, which was filled with the flaming recovery vehicle, its crane drooping to the ground and twisted like a pretzel. Before the enormity of the event was processed in his frontal cortex, the M1's turret rang with the impact of a tank round. The viewfinder filled with the soft white glow of dozens of enemy tanks pouring in from the north. The M1 rocked back and forth as another round found the hull side. Then another.

The interior lights flickered then went out. Harland's first instinct was to get out, but the training quelled the rising panic within. The safest place in combat was inside the tank. The worst thing you could do was leave the safety of its protective armor. The only thing left to do was fight. It was okay. This was going to be just like that game in the arcade. You put the quarter in, and you fired until it was Game Over.

He took a deep breath and scooted over to the loader's seat. One knee pressed against the button. The door slid open, and he grabbed a SABOT round from the ready rack. An alarm shrieked somewhere in the tank, and smoke started to fill up the turret. Seconds later, fire suppressant flooded around the compartment as he guided the tip of the round into the gunner's breech. The stench of burnt electronics filled the turret, and he moved back to his seat after slamming the breech shut. Another round lashed the tank, and he took control of the gun, aiming manually for the nearest tank. There it was - its big ugly black turret sticking out at him. Just another wireframe target. He'd get a bonus tank at 15,000 points, so there was nothing to worry about. Today, he was going for the high score.

The world went black.

CHECKMATE

Colonel Mackinsky was halfway over the Fulda River when he got the news. Objective Rook had finally been taken. Well, praise be and pass the grits. Did Captain Harris want an achievement award? Queen and King had been captured no less than five minutes ago. While the tanks were waiting, Bravo Company was taking its sweet time assaulting a podunk hamlet protected by a handful of Russians who weren't even good enough to be sent up to the front lines. Apparently, Harris had not gotten the memo about the need for speed during what was supposed to have been a "lightning" assault.

He shouldn't have been so surprised. Bravo's company commander had fumbled the ball from the start of the operation. First, his APCs had been late getting over the bridge. When they finally did arrive near Rook, missile and RPG fire had taken out two of Delta's tanks. Attempts to minimize civilian casualties had slowed down the assault even further. By the time the end was in sight, the battle to the east of the city had long been decided, and the shock of the initial attack had surely worn off. Delta's two tank platoons at Queen had eliminated the antique T-55s of the 247th Guards Motorized Rifle Regiment's Third Battalion. At this point in time, the unit had been relegated to the scrap heap of military history - but not without putting up a fight. The infantry had managed to mount a staunch defense on the reverse slope of Hill 228, which had cost a pair of Abrams.

To make matters worse, the follow-on reinforcements from 8th Infantry Division were nowhere to be seen yet, and no one seemed to know where they were. Mackinsky's task force had its pants around its ankles and its butt in the wind. How long would it be before someone came along and kicked it? It was time to consolidate his gains. He spoke slowly over the radio, hoping to keep the jitters out of his voice.

BEARCLAW TO ALL ELEMENTS. DIG IN IMMEDIATELY AND WAIT FOR REINFORCEMENTS TO ARRIVE. MAINTAIN RADIO SILENCE EXCEPT FOR SPOT REPORTS, OVER.

The armored ambulances shot past him going the other direction. Mackinsky had set up a temporary field hospital on the west bank, and all afternoon, the vehicles had been shuttling back and forth. Most of the casualties were infantry casualties from Bravo's assault on Rook. A trickle of civilians had come back too. When Clifton had given him a casualty report update, Mackinsky ordered him to leave them out of the equation. Losing focus now would cost him dearly.

By the time his M-113 reached the east bank of the Fulda River, he was flooded with reports from Delta's commander.

DELTA TO BEARCLAW, WE ARE IN CONTACT WITH MULTIPLE REPEAT MULTIPLE TANGO EIGHT ZEROS TO THE NORTH OF QUEEN. TAKING CASUALTIES. REQUEST PERMISSION TO WITHDRAW, OVER.

The air fell out of Mackinsky's lungs. Time had run out, and the whole operation was in jeopardy. He slapped a balled fist into his palm, sensing that the initiative had passed over to the Russians.

BEARCLAW MAIN TO DELTA. GIVE ME A QUICK RUNDOWN OF YOUR SITUATION AND THE NUMBERS YOU ARE FACING, OVER.

Over to the east, salvos of gunfire blared across the land. No answer came back from Delta's commander over the net. Were they overrun completely or were they too heavily engaged in combat? He had a platoon of tanks and a handful of Bradleys sitting over at King. Surely, they'd be able to see what was happening. Why hadn't they reported in? A quick call to the commander revealed why - they were in heavy contact with a company of T-80s.

The first M1 from Delta came roaring back over the nearest hill ten seconds later followed by another one. Mackinsky's entire body shook with rage. After all the time spent in exercises practicing orderly retreats and covering fire, the unit had fallen back without discipline. The colonel shouted orders to his driver and the command APC shot forward to meet the Abrams pulling back into Lüdermünd. The only way he could force down his anger was to speak to the combat team around King. By now, he had a more complete picture of what was happening.

Three companies of enemy tanks were now engaged with the task force. A handful of Abrams and Bradleys to the east had managed to pin down and delay two platoons worth of T-80s to the north of King. The rest of the enemy tanks were headed directly for Rook and would be on them any second. Mackinsky's APC shot into the north of the town moments before the first shots managed to crash down into Lüdermünd. One of the Abrams from Delta sat uselessly in the middle of an intersection, its turret turned away from the onrushing vehicles. Mackinsky ordered his driver to stop just short of the tank. Over the din of gunfire, he screamed at the tank's commander and gestured wildly to the east. The words came out as a garble, but the sergeant got the point and ducked down into the Abrams. While Mackinsky's APC passed by, the gun spat out an anti-tank round.

A soupy mixture of strained voices stepped over each other on the battalion net. Mackinsky cleared it with a few choice words, and a tense silence replaced the near panic. From the sound of it, the team near King was now isolated from the rest of the task force with Soviet tanks sitting between them and Rook. The company commander assured them they could hold out. With what little time he had left, Mackinsky decided to muster a hasty defense around Lüdermünd.

Captain Harris was found to the east of the town, having already dug in his troops without being ordered. The move had salvaged what little regard the colonel had for the company commander. LAWs had been passed out like candy to the exhausted troops, and one of three Dragons had claimed a kill already.

Collectively, it wasn't enough to hold off a company of enemy tanks, but Bravo's morale was high after taking their objective, and the men were determined not to give it up without a damned hard fight.

A platoon of Abrams was all that he had left to keep Rook from falling. He spaced them out evenly along the eastern perimeter of the town and hoped the Russians wouldn't figure out just how thin he had spread out his defenses. With no reserve, all it would take was a quick concentrated thrust at the flanks to reveal his hand. If the Soviet commander had any brains, he would probe the perimeter early on. If that happened, he had already made up his mind to pop as much smoke as he could and withdraw west over the nearby bridge then blow it. His tanks near King would be sacrificed, but the rest of them would live to fight another day.

Captain Rogers, the artillery officer in the FIST vehicle, had moved mountains to gather what little support was available. With an excited smile, he informed Mackinsky there were two fire missions available from the one five five howitzers to the west. Did he want him to call in one? Mackinsky's head bobbed up and down like a drinking duck.

"Hell yes!"

It wasn't long before the main body of the Russian tank force showed up. The T-80s poured along the flat stretch of farmland that lay nestled between the hills to the east of the town. They came in a long line abreast, firing wildly as they approached. Mackinsky's insides tightened into a cramp as he watched them rush forward like beasts. There was no covering fire or leapfrogging tactics - just an arrogant onslaught of men and vehicles from a commander unconcerned about preserving his forces. The town behind him crumbled under the weight of incoming fire. Chunks of buildings sagged and fell over while facades were shed like skins.

Each time an Abrams destroyed a T-80, the oncoming tanks answered with volleys of fire that landed increasingly closer as the range between them decreased. After twenty seconds, every single American tank had suffered at least one hit. Soon enough, their turrets resembled the bruised and battered faces of prize fighters after a dozen rounds with the heavyweight contender.

Mackinsky's track suffered a glancing blow from a round that killed the driver and kindled a fire that forced him to jump off and climb into the FIST vehicle.

"Where's that fire mission?" he shouted to Rogers. The artillery officer slid a map towards him and dropped the handset.

"You're danger close with these tanks. You sure you want it called in now?"

Mackinsky ran a hand over his rough pockmarked face. What choice did he have?

"Call it in."

He grabbed a headset in the back of the rig and tuned into the battalion frequency.

BEARCLAW TO ALL ELEMENTS NEAR ROOK. PULL BACK. INCOMING FIRE MISSION. PULL BACK AND FIND COVER IMMEDIATELY, OVER.

The ground trembled and heaved like water as the artillery splashed down all around the outskirts of the town. Mackinsky and Rogers hugged the floor of the FIST as each round hammered into the earth like the fist of an angry god. Once or twice, the vehicle actually bounced off the ground. He had never felt so powerless in all his life. Mackinsky prayed for each ear-shattering drumbeat of high explosive to be the last one. The FIST vehicle rolled on its side at one point, sending boxes of ammunition and radio equipment tumbling. Both Rogers and the task force commander were flung at the nearest wall. If he had not been so terrified at that point, Mackinsky might have laughed. After all, he had done this to himself. For once, there was no one else to blame.

Mercifully, the barrage stopped after what felt like hours. When Mackinsky opened the hatch, he found everything coated in a thick layer of dust. Three hundred meters east of the town, the green fields and farmland had been transformed into a moonscape. The group of trees that marked the halfway point between Rook and Knight had been obliterated, and all that was left to mark their presence was a line of blackened stumps.

Three or four enemy tanks were on fire, and one looked like it had been crushed by a direct shell hit. One of the Abrams that was poking out just a little too far east of Bravo's main defensive line had a chunk of its turret caved in.

For what felt like a solid minute, nothing moved or fired, and a chill breeze swept through the dusty land. The place felt like an old Western town just before a gunfight. A single bead of sweat wormed its way down Mackinsky's face just before the next shot rang out. He didn't see who fired it, but the effect was instant.

The remnants of the T-80s, now somewhere at two platoons, let loose on the pair of M1 Abrams that were protecting the town. A rain of armored-piercing rounds struck the turrets and hulls. Despite the deep scars that marked each impact, the American tanks kept firing back. When two of the T-80s managed to break through the tight perimeter of infantry, one of them managed to destroy an Abrams with a shot to the rear turret that penetrated the ammunition compartment. Even then, the American crew bailed out with only minor injuries. Two of them managed to make it into the protective cover of the town while the other pair were cut down by machine gun fire from the enemy tanks.

Mackinsky called again and again over the radio, hoping to raise the combat team near King. Last he heard, they were fighting for their lives eight kilometers to the east, surrounded by enemy tanks and cut off from the main body of the task force here at Rook. Now his desperate pleas for a sitrep went unanswered, and he could only assume the worst. No one was coming to the rescue. A quick look over his shoulder revealed that the fighting had entered the town. Harris had reported that the Dragons were gone and they were down to one LAW per squad. With the rest of the 8th Infantry Division sitting uselessly behind the hills to the west, there seemed little to do except choose between certain destruction at the hands of the enemy or an orderly retreat.

Well, at least it wouldn't be a total wash. The engineers reported in that the bridge to the southwest of Lüdermünd and the bridge to the east of Hemmen were both wired to blow.

BEARCLAW TO ALL ELEMENTS. POP SMOKE AND PULL BACK SOUTHWEST OVER THE BRIDGE IMMEDIATELY. REPEAT. ALL FORCES WITHDRAW TO RALLY POINT ZEBRA.

An incoming smoke fire mission would help to cover the remnants of the task force as it pulled back.

Mackinsky watched in despair as the Soviet tanks poured into town and his APCs withdrew into the wall of fog that spread like a blanket over the devastated landscape. The failures here would have to be accounted for in good order, and they were his to own entirely. Next time, he would do better - if there were a next time.

ABOUT THE AUTHOR

Brad Smith is a freelance writer and game designer. He has a keen interest in the topic of the late Cold War, which has fed his creative output. He has authored around a dozen books set in an alternate World War III: 1985 universe. His blog can be found at: www.hexsides.com. You can also access his books on the Amazon.com store page. Several of his stories are available through Lock 'n Load Publishing.

His main interests are writing, wargaming, and spending time with his wife and son. He recently designed "NATO Air Commander" and the soon to be released "That Others May Live" both published by Hollandspiele. Two of his favorite wargames are "Gulf Strike" and "The Korean War" from Victory Games. His gaming blog can be found at: www.hexsides.blogspot.com.

Brad has worked as an Emergency Medical Responder in Canada then as a writer based in Geneva, Switzerland before moving to Japan in 2004, where he has lived ever since. He holds a Bachelor's degree majoring in History from the University of Winnipeg, a Master's in Journalism from the University of British Columbia, and a dual Master's degree in TESOL and Applied Linguistics from the University of Leicester. He has written for academic journals, newspapers, radio, and magazines on a variety of topics. He recently served as an editor for an issue of Yaah! magazine and is a frequent contributor to other game journals.

His main writing inspirations include Tom Clancy, Joe Scalzi, Ralph Peters, and Stephen King. His favorite books include "Red Storm Rising", "Old Man's War", and "Red Army".

ABOUT THE EDITOR
- Hans Korting -

I have been reading books about (military) aviation history all of my life, and this way the connection with military history is easily made. Main interest is WWII, but I also enjoy reading up on and playing games about WWI, modern-era warfare, the American Civil War, Napoleonics, and more. First game ever was bought in an American book store in Amsterdam, Avalon Hill's D-Day '77. Next game was SPI's Arnhem, and a whole range of games has followed since. Putting my hands, or rather eyes, where my mouth is, I next decided to help out proofreading rulebooks. Some gaming magazines were next, like War Diary magazine. I also write about boardwargames for Ducosim's (DutchConflictSimulation) Spel! magazine, and sometimes try to write a decent article for a magazine too. Daytime job is at a small insurance broker as a claims handler.

AUDIO BOOK EDITION
- Narrated By: Keith Tracton -

Keith Tracton has been acting in some way, shape, or form for thirty-seven years. A veteran of stage, screen, TV, film, voiceovers and, of course, audiobook narration. His audiobooks can be found on iTunes and on Audible.com. The only thing he has been doing longer than acting is playing board war games - forty-four years doing that, and still going strong. As such, he also very much considers himself fortunate to be the lead developer for Lock 'n Load Publishing's upcoming alternate-WWIII platoon level game series **World At War 85**.

WHAT IS THE WORLD AT WAR 85 GAME SERIES
- by David Heath -

I am the Director of Operations at Lock 'n Load Publishing, where we produce both tabletop and computer games with a strategy theme. So what made us publish a book of short stories? The love of gaming. These short stories were inspired by the kind of stories friends share about games they played and the adventures they experienced while playing them. Those stories always remind me of the kind told by my Dad, his friends, and my own buddies who spent time in the service.

The idea for this book series started from a long desire to hear the stories of other gamers, and to share my love for gaming. This project became real thanks to Brad Smith, Hans Korting, Keith Tracton, and many others. Without their support this never would have happened. While talking this over it became clear we weren't the only ones who enjoyed telling and listening to gaming adventures.

This story use a number of things from our World at War 85 game series, specifically the names units and even the occasional moments inspired by game events. This added a new level to our stories and added the ability and similarity for these men to live on in each of our games.

Some of you may be wondering what the World at War 85 game series is all about. The World at War 85 (WaW85) series is a dynamic platoon-level tactical combat board game series centered on armored combat from the 1980s in a fictional World War III setting. With unparalleled artwork and a formation based game mechanic that keeps both players constantly involved, each action-packed engagement plays out cinematically. Decisions need to be made quickly. Tactical leadership is key. Unique abilities and synergies enhance effectiveness. And detailed objectives based ont he scenario layout encourages bold gameplay. There is even a Solo module for those quiet nights at home.

Platoon combat is central to WaW85, but besides Heavy Armor and Soft Armor units, we have Support Weapon such as mortars, heavy machine guns, and anti-tank guns. There are also Helicopters, faction Leaders, fixed-wing Close Air Support and an in depth suit of Artillery options, both on and off-board. Individuals such as Leaders, Special Weapons Teams, and, of course, Special Forces, complete the forces available for each side. We also have free downloadable game walkthroughs, making the game series more accessible to new players more than ever.

Whether you are a fan of 80s-era military fiction or the World War 3 setting, the WaW85 series has you covered with a variety of boxed games and expansions, including an evolving storyline to follow as you play through ear game in the series. With WaW85 the gaming never ends. It's Platoon-level tactical combat at its best!

WORLD AT WAR 85 NOVELS

SOMETHING THE SOVIETS DIDN'T PLAN ON

It is May 1985 and World War III rages in Central Europe. Fledgling insurgent groups in the East Bloc fight for independence from their Soviet overlords. America pledges to help. Among the teams of US military advisers are two Vietnam War veterans, sent in to assist an East German major named Werner Brandt and his motley band of fighters. Their objectives are to help destroy Soviet military reinforcements as they speed towards the frontlines and to eliminate the Russian garrison in control of Saxony. It won't be easy – Brandt is consumed with a lust for vengeance that threatens to derail his own operations.

Captain Joe Ricci and Sergeant Ned Littlejohn are about to enter a combat zone for the first time in nearly fifteen years. With them, they bring the scarred memories of their Vietnam experiences. As the stakes climb higher and the battle to survive grows more intense, each decision could lead to the liberation of a nation or their own downfall.

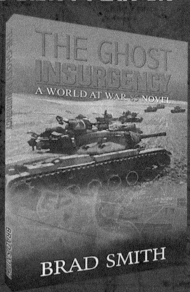

BRAD SMITH

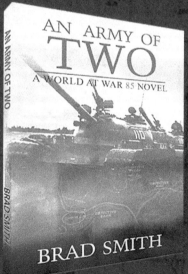

BRAD SMITH

THE SOVIET INVASION CONTINUES

First Lieutenant Darren White is trapped behind enemy lines with the remnants of his cavalry troop. Together with his second-in-command, Maurice Fitzgerald, he waits for the right opportunity to strike back at the Russians in occupied West Germany.

As they conduct joint operations with a Special Forces team in the Fulda Gap, a terrible secret is uncovered. The Soviets have found a sure-fire way to win the war. It's up to White and Fitzgerald to stop them. A daring operation might just be enough to make or break the Soviet war effort in Fulda. Will Fitzgerald and White's personal differences doom the attempt?

LOCK 'N LOAD PUBLISHING
WWW.LNLPUBLISHING.COM

STORMING THE GAP

WORLD AT WAR 85

World War III has Begun

STORMING THE GAP is the first volume in the new WORLD AT WAR 85 SERIES, a line of games centered on fast and furious platoon-level combat. Set in an alternate history 1985, the globe is thrust into the maelstrom of World War III when the Warsaw Pact armies storm across the border between East and West Germany in a gamble to seize West Germany, and the whole of Free Europe.

Fight the opening battles of World War III; from desperate delaying actions by US Armored Cavalry and West German Panzergrenadier forces to determined counterattacks by local ad-hoc armored forces against the might of the Soviet hordes. Strike fast with Soviet Air Assault troops in heliborne ops, securing roadways to allow the massed armor columns of the PACT to sweep westward into Germany. The devastating armed forces of West Germany, the United States, East Germany, and the Soviet Union are at your disposal in your quest to reshape the world and history.

The weight of the tactical decisions rests solely on your shoulders. Can NATO slow the Soviet advance with the armor and infantry they can bring to bear? Or skillfully use Close Air Support and Attack Helicopter units to swing the tide of battle in your favor? Can the PACT slice through into Germany and cross the Rhine river, gateway to the conquest of all of Europe?

LOCK 'N LOAD
PUBLISHING
WWW.LNLPUBLISHING.COM

STORMING THE GAP EXPANSION
WORLD AT WAR 85

The war expands!

Welcome to the Expansion Pack for Storming the Gap. Inside, you find 3 complete modules to expand the scope of your game. You'll also find Data cards to reference each unit in World at War 85, and conversions to play it on a tabletop:

The Breakthrough to Frankfurt
Want to fight with your World at War 85 forces on maps of a real section of the Fulda Gap, near Frankfurt West Germany, and adapted specifically for World at War 85 play? The Defense of Frankfurt module has sixteen maps.

Storm and Steel Second Wave!
Storm and Steel Second Wave is an expansion based on the action and forces in the novel Storm an dSteel Second Wave! It adds TWO NEW COUNTER SHEETS, 60+ FORMATION CARDS, and THREE NEW MAPS to your World at War 85 forces.

The Drive to Giessen!
The Drive on Giessen is a campaign game for World at War 85 that allows the generation and play of a set of linked game scenarios depicting a Soviet division's drive across West Germany against NATO forces.

LOCK 'N LOAD PUBLISHING
WWW.LNLPUBLISHING.COM

HEROES AGAINST THE RED STAR

The Red Star Strikes!

It's the spring of 1985 and the Cold War has turned Hot. Out of the dawn sky, Soviet paratroopers are being whisked across the West German border. On the ground, the 1st Tank Division and 33rd Motor Rifle Regiment are rolling toward key command-and-control targets. NATO has to mobilize quickly. World War III has begun, and once again Western Europe is the focal point.

In Heroes Against the Red Star, the Lock 'n Load Tactical Series presents the sweeping rush of the Soviet Red Army, from the shock of the ambitious opening offensive on May 14th against American-held positions in West Germany to the furious rush to Paris, in June, against emboldened French forces

LOCK 'N LOAD
PUBLISHING
WWW.LNLPUBLISHING.COM

CPSIA information can be obtained
at www.ICGtesting.com
Printed in the USA
LVHW051638180421
684849LV00010B/301